sleepless

Also by

CYN BALOG

FAIRY TALE

sleepless

CYN BALOG

Delacorte Press

Copyright © 2010 by Cyn Balog

All rights reserved. Published in the United States by Delacorte Press,
an imprint of Random House Children's Books,
a division of Random House, Inc., New York.

Delacorte Press is a registered trademark and the colophon is a trademark of
Random House, Inc.

Visit us on the Web! www.randomhouse.com/teens

Educators and librarians, for a variety of teaching tools,
visit us at www.randomhouse.com/teachers

Library of Congress Cataloging-in-Publication data is available upon request.
ISBN 978-0-385-73848-4 (hc) – ISBN 978-0-385-90733-0 (lib. bdg.) –
ISBN 978-0-375-89493-0 (e-book)

The text of this book is set in 11-point Baskerville Book.

Book design by Marci Senders

Printed in the United States of America

10 9 8 7 6 5 4 3 2

First Edition

For Sara and Gabrielle,

who made every sleepless night worth it

ACKNOWLEDGMENTS

Working on *Sleepless* has been like a dream because of some very special people. As always, thank you to my writing BFF, Mandy Hubbard or Amanda Grace or whatever she goes by these days, who is the definition of persistence and determination and the reason I've been able to keep a positive outlook even on the very bleakest days. Thank you also to my many talented writer friends who have helped me over the past few months, including Brooke Taylor, Josh Berk, Keri Mikulski, Carrie Ryan, Saundra Mitchell, Aprilynne Pike, Michelle Zink, Maggie Stiefvater, Cynthia Leitich Smith, Teri Brown, Heather Dearly, and Cheryl Mansfield. You are all amazing.

Thank you to my agent, Jim McCarthy, and to Stephanie Elliott, Krista Vitola, and the rest of the people at Delacorte Press who had a role in bringing *Sleepless* to life. It has been such a pleasure working with all of you.

To my parents, Marilynn and Richard Reilly, thanks for everything. Thank you also to my mother-in-law, Gail Balog, for babysitting and for promotional efforts, and to the rest of my family. A big thank-you to my grandfather, Orlando Bianco, whose own Ellis Island story served as the basis for Eron's background, and to my mother for telling it to me.

Big hugs to anyone who has read my books or come out to support me at any of my events—I wouldn't be able to do this without you. Your e-mails and letters keep me going every day and are treasured more than you can possibly know.

Special shout-out to anyone named Kiki. Your name isn't really goofy. Try going through life with a last name that sounds like a character from *The Hobbit*.

And I've saved the best for last. Thank you to Bri, Bun, and Brie, who are the reason behind everything good in my life. The moon for you.

Griffin Colburn knew something was wrong the moment he slid into the driver's seat.

It was a twinge. Nothing more. He shook his head, blinked. Pushed it off.

His Mustang started fine, like always. He revved the engine a few times, like always. He always said it was to keep it from stalling, which it sometimes did in cold weather, but really he loved to feel the power behind the car. It was old, but still fast and dangerous.

He wouldn't know how dangerous, though, until that night.

As he backed out of the driveway, Julia blew him a long, exaggerated stage kiss, as if he were shipping off to war. As if she knew she'd never see him again. Then she wiped some nonexistent tears from her eyes and pretended to sob hysterically into her hands. His headlights illuminated her slight, pale body, crowned with long reddish hair. She squinted in their glow and then smiled toothily, like a preschooler.

He fed a Sinatra disc into his CD player and grinned back at her, then listened as Ol' Blue Eyes crooned, "Someday, when I'm awfully low." The tinkling of the piano keys drowned out the screeching of his tires, and as he began to sing along, he felt it, fiercer now. It started in his temples, *trailed behind his eyes, the momentary shiver that comes somewhere between wakefulness and sleep.* Twinge. Twinge. *For a second, he felt as if he were falling. He blinked again, gripped the steering wheel to steady himself.* Twinge.

This time, he squeezed his eyes closed, only for a moment. In that moment, the image of the beautiful young woman appeared.

Whoa, he thought. Too many late nights. He sat up in the driver's seat, stretched his spine. Usually when his mind wandered, it went to NFL play-offs. Or to the scantily clad, Playboy Playmate type of beauty. And yet, when he blinked again, he could see her, as plainly as if she were sitting in the passenger seat next to him. She was dressed in the pink silk of a fairy-tale princess, braiding her black waist-length hair. When she batted her heavy lashes, a slow smile spread on her face.

Then her eyes focused on him. Shark's eyes, two emotionless black buttons.

He shook his head, rubbed one temple with his free hand, checked the seat beside him again. Nothing but his baseball glove and a grease-stained fast-food bag. I definitely need more sleep, he thought as he sped out of the neighborhood. He was halfway down Peasant when he felt a slow, warm caress run up his neck, down his chest—twinge. His whole body lurched forward. It was almost like he skipped forward a few moments in time. He must have driven right through that stop sign on Peasant, because he couldn't remember coming up to it. Instead, he found himself on Main Street, at an amber light, which normally he would have sped through, but sensing something was off, he slowed. Suddenly—twinge—he blinked and it was green again, without ever having turned red.

"What the . . ." He gripped the wheel tighter.

He thought about turning back, but only for a second. Griffin Colburn didn't have a reputation for spinelessness.

Just a few more minutes. Just a few more minutes and I'll be in bed. He pressed down on the accelerator, thinking of home.

He blinked again. Twinge.

And she was there.

This time, clearer.

Beckoning to him.

CHAPTER 1
Julia

"You can ring my be-e-ell, ring my bell!"

My eyes flicker open. All I see is a pink satin pillow, which I've clamped over my face to block out the rest of the world. When I remove it, I recoil in the morning sunlight like the undead and crane my neck to check the clock at my bedside.

9:20 a.m. *Oh, hell no.*

Before I can theorize who on earth hates me enough to be playing cheesy disco music on the only day of the week I can sleep in, I realize that the noise is coming from under my other pillow. Grinding my teeth, I rip the pillow off the bed, throw it across the room, and see my cell phone vibrating there.

Griffin.

He'd been quiet for all of three minutes during our "study session" the night before, while I was fixing him cookies and milk, which was plenty of time for him to reprogram my phone with music he knew would make me want to hurl. I quickly pick the phone up; the display says "private." I know only one person who has a private number, all the easier to annoy me with. This is, without a doubt, the last time I'll ever play Betty Crocker for him.

As I flip the cell open, my eyes trail to the floor, where I've thrown the proofs of our picture from prom. I'd been convinced I looked like a princess in that photograph, until he proudly showed me the proofs last night. He'd had his pointer and middle fingers behind me, giving me rabbit ears. Jerk. "What?" I groan.

"Ms. Devine?" The voice is professional, kind of effeminate . . . but I'm smarter than that. Griffin can disguise his voice better than anyone.

"Yeah?"

"Coby Baker from the *Bucks County Courier Times.*"

I sigh. This is a good one. Last weekend, I won a major cash award from Publishers Clearinghouse, which was just too obvious, since I'm not that lucky. "And?" I snuggle back under the covers.

"Are you Julia Devine, Griffin Colburn's girlfriend?"

"Who?" I ask innocently. There's silence on the other end; I've caught him off guard, a small victory for me. "Yeah, I am. What about him?"

"I was hoping I could get a quote from you, as his girlfriend."

Oh, I can give you a quote, I think, but I doubt any paper would be able to publish it.

I'm silent, choosing the words, when his voice comes through again, more serious. "I'm sorry for your loss, Ms. Devine."

"Oh," I say, thinking fast. "I thought this was about him robbing the 7-E again. Did he finally croak?"

5

"Um . . . a-are you . . . ," the voice stammers. "The car accident?"

"Oh, *right,*" I say. Wow, Griffin is pulling out all the stops today. "It slipped my mind. Okay. Let's see. He was a really nice guy, except for that weird fungus. And the funny smell. He was always taking chances. Clearly he is responsible for his own undoing." I pause. "How's that?"

More silence. This is where I expect Griffin to break in with his usual "What's up?" Instead, "Coby," still businesslike, says, "Um . . . thank you, Ms. Devine."

"Pug, it's nine in the morning," I begin, but then I notice the words "call ended" flashing on the display.

Huh.

I toss the phone aside and slip deeper under my comforter. Ten minutes later, I'm almost asleep when it happens again.

"You can ring my be-e-ell, ring my bell!"

Cursing, I find the phone tangled within my sheets and check the screen. Private, again. My first and only boyfriend is *so* dead.

I flip the phone open. "Yeah?" I say, grouchier this time.

"Ms. Devine?"

"Who are you now, the *Wall Street Journal*?"

"Actually, it's the *Intelligencer.*"

Okay, now this has gone too far. "Do you want a quote from the victim's girlfriend, too?" I ask, my voice saccharine.

"If it wouldn't be too much trouble."

"Actually," I say, "it's a lot of trouble. Pug, I'm trying to sleep. This. Is. Not. Funny."

"Hey. Julia Devine." The voice on the other end sparkles with recognition. "You're *the* Julia Devine. The one who made all those headlines. Right? How long ago was that? Five years ago?"

I bite my lip, suddenly aware of my heart thudding against my camisole. If there's anything, any topic in my life, that Griffin knows is off-limits, it's that. Even *he* wouldn't touch it. "Nine," I whisper.

There's silence on the other end. "Ms. Devine," the voice finally says, "have you not heard about the accident?"

My voice is a squeak. "Accident?"

"Ms. Devine. There was an accident, on Main Street, last night. Griffin Colburn was killed."

It seems I was right about one thing, I realize as I flip the phone shut without another word and numbly stare at the display.

My first and only boyfriend *is* so dead.

CHAPTER 2
Eron

If Mama, God rest her soul, could see me now, crouching outside the window of a girl's house, in this tree, she would surely rise from her grave and swat the life clean out of me. And I agree with her; this is no place for a man. But that is one thing I am not.

At least, not yet.

Watching the bedtime ritual of a woman from a clandestine post is perfectly acceptable behavior for us Sleepbringers, known as Sandmen to humans. In fact, I watch more than one woman every night. I'm sure Mama would get out the belt if she knew that. It's not proper human behavior, so it was a struggle even for me to grasp. After all, I still *appear* human, and one's human sensibilities are difficult simply to disregard. Even now I'm not entirely comfortable with stalking women in the dark, though I've been carrying out this seduction for nearly a hundred years. I'm about as used to it as I'll ever be.

When I died and made my choice to join the Sleepbringers, it was Mama I thought of. She was the only one I hated to leave behind—well, besides Gertie, perhaps. Without me, Mama was alone. I was only seventeen, and I had aspirations to be someone, to make something out of my life. But all too suddenly, that was over. I was a picker in a textile mill in Newark and snagged my shoulder in one of the machines as I was trying to free some bunched fabric. Tore my arm up dreadfully, and by the time they got me to the hospital, I'd lost too much blood. It didn't hurt. Or perhaps it did. I can't remember. Like I said, it was a hundred years ago.

I do remember, like yesterday, sitting in a dream state and talking to a beautiful young woman. She told me not to be afraid, and it felt as if I'd met her before, perhaps in my dreams. For the first time, I didn't trip over my words, didn't make a fool of myself like I always did with the fairer sex. I was comfortable with her. Little did I know that as I spoke to this young woman, she was drawing me further and further into her world, seducing me, and pulling me forever away from the simple life I'd known as Eron DeMarchelle, textile picker from Newark, New Jersey. By the time she explained to me that my life was over, there was nothing left to be done.

Julia is sitting at her vanity, applying some cream to her skin. If I could speak to her, I would protest; her skin is already the color and texture of Ivory soap. Perfect. That is, except for the three small purple scars, like a cat scratch, on her right cheek. She always wears her reddish hair down. It looks lovely when it spills upon her satin pillows, but during the day, it covers too much of her face, which I suppose is her objective. She has always been wildly self-conscious about those scars, which she received when she was seven, in an incident she has otherwise done a wonderful job of forgetting.

Her eyelids sag heavily, so my job should be easy today. For some reason, the thought saddens me.

I'm woken from my reverie when the room suddenly goes dark. I strain to see through the glass the covers of Julia's bed floating down upon her small frame. Time to begin.

Stepping into the room, I adjust my cuff links and pat my coat pockets to ensure I have a good supply of sand in them. I pass the collection of running trophies, the posters and models of architectural masterpieces, the dusty shelves of discarded stuffed animals she cuddled faithfully when she was a child. Julia is on her side. I peer over her and realize that she's holding a frame in her hands. Julia's bureau is covered with framed photographs of family and friends; she feels safe with them watching her. In the darkness, I can't see the picture she's holding beneath the glass. I spread the sand over her, and before my ritual is anywhere near completion, she's dreaming away. She turns onto her back and mumbles something I can't quite make out.

Julia often talks in her sleep, and usually, her words are laced with worry. She speaks things in her dreams that she is afraid to say while conscious. She is quiet, prefers to keep to herself, which is something I've always understood, because I was quite the same way. When she was younger, she was the most precocious, talkative child I had ever known, but she's much more tentative now, as if she no longer believes that her thoughts have worth. I want to soothe her, but that would break the first rule of the Sleepbringers: once the human is asleep, we must make our exit. Quickly, I leave the way I came, but I can't bring myself to move on to my other charges right away. I sit on a branch and attempt to find her form in the darkened room, but all I can see is my reflection in the glass.

"Hello, my pet," a voice breathes, tickling my ear.

"Good evening, Chimere," I whisper. I don't need to turn to know that it is my mentor. A hundred years has bred a familiarity I didn't know possible. She is that beautiful young woman I spoke about—well, if one could call her a woman; she is not human, either. Though, the difference between us is that she never has been and never will be. I've almost come to take for granted that she will forever be in my life. It's hard to believe that in another few weeks, I will never see her again.

Chimere peers through the window. "Ah! Of course. This one shall be the hardest for you to part with, no doubt."

"What makes you say that?" I ask, finally looking at her. She carefully adjusts her white petticoats and absently begins to braid her waist-length black hair. It's one of her most endearing habits.

She smiles at me, her eyes saying, *Must you even ask?* "You two have been through much together."

"That's of no importance. It's not as though she realizes that," I mutter darkly.

"It matters to you, though, does it not? I can always guess where to find you. Most often when I come to check on you, you're in this very spot."

I don't answer. Perhaps I was spending a few extra moments outside Julia's bedroom, but I hardly felt it noticeable.

She smiles again. "It's not at all unexpected. This one replaced your beloved, after all."

I hitch a shoulder. Yes, Gertie was the girl I loved when I

was seventeen, though it's hard to think of her as that. "Beloved" would suggest a closeness I hadn't achieved with the choirgirl from my church. In fact, we had never touched, or even spoken to one another. I firmly doubt she even knew my name. We only exchanged glances and smiles back and forth across the pews at St. Ann's Church every Sunday for a year. Before the accident, I'd made plans to ask her to the church social. Since then, I've spent a hundred years regretting not following through with those plans. "Beloved" sounds rather presumptuous.

That is one of the reasons I agreed to join Chimere; Chimere had told me that if I joined her for "a spell" and served her well, I could continue my life as a human. She said that every one of us Sandmen had unfinished business, and I was certain that Gertie was mine. She also told me that if I became a Sandman, I could lull dear Gertie to sleep every night. Yes, I could be closer to her than I ever had been as a human. But time passes quickly among our people, and I had no inkling that the "spell" Chimere spoke of was equal to a lifetime in human years. When Gertie died at the age of ninety-six, after being married to another (almost too much for me to bear) and having many children and grandchildren, I mourned her as if she were my beloved, despite my being little more than a glimmer in her vast scrapbook of memories. But I accepted it. After all, that is what we Sleepbringers must learn to do: put the safety and happiness of our charges ahead of our own. It was enough to see her living a good life, even without me in it.

After Gertie's passing, I was given Julia. She was only a

baby when I first met her, a smiling, redheaded little bundle who much preferred chewing on the railing of her crib to my visits.

Chimere says, "Our people always seem to have a fondness for the one who takes our beloved's place."

In body, Chimere is only sixteen. But she has thousands of years of wisdom about the Sandmen, enough that I sometimes think of her as a mother hen. I can never argue with her logic. "Yes, I suppose."

"Well, are you ready?" she says, pouting.

In a few weeks, my obligation to the Sleepbringers will be fulfilled, and I will be able to continue the life I left a hundred years ago. In truth, though I am excited, I am a wreck about the whole thing. Among the countless other worries, I imagine that the world has changed quite a bit since I left it.

"I suppose. Was my replacement called up?"

She nods. "Yes. He agreed. And he is Julia's beloved, so I think it will work nicely."

I can't help bristling. Julia has a beloved? Most often, I learn these things through the dreams of my charges, but Julia has never dreamt consistently enough of one person for me to think she has a special attachment. Julia doesn't dream often, and when she does, she is usually alone. She dreams of places, of mountainous buildings of steel and glass. Julia is much different from the rest of the women I've been charged with. Like me, she feels more content among beautiful works of architecture than around people. I've always thought she'd be forever searching—like I was when I was alive—for a kindred spirit, one soul to understand her.

I think of the silver frame she's holding, and her eyelids, sagging, I realize now, not so much from fatigue but from grief. Her *beloved*. "And when will I be expected to begin his training?"

"In time. He's still getting accustomed to his new powers," she explains.

I look back through the window, at Julia. It's almost unbelievable that in another few months, I will no longer be in those dreams of hers, beside her, staring up at buildings whose roofs touch the moon. I will be human, like her, and yet she will not know me at all; the gap between us will be immeasurable. Insurmountable. "All right," I say, trying to keep my nerves quelled.

"You are worried, no doubt, about the training?" Chimere asks, studying my eyes. "Do not be. It's very rare that a replacement cannot fulfill his duties."

"But it does happen," I murmur.

"Well, yes . . . but so? It's not as though this life has been all that torturous for you, has it?"

"Of course not, but after one hundred years of the same . . . it tends to be a bit . . ."

She grins. "Tedious. I have heard that before."

"I have no idea how you've done it for so many thousands of years."

"You forget. I was never human. Maybe it is that I do not know what I am missing," she says. "You do want to be human, do you not? To finish that which has been left undone?"

"Of course. More than anything. Though I still do not know what my unfinished business is."

"It will become clear to you, in time." She clasps her hands together and inspects me. "Is there anything else troubling you? As you know, the further you proceed in your training of your replacement, the more human you will become. As he accepts your duties, you will gradually become human. At first you may be human for only a few minutes a day, but eventually that time will stretch, until you are completely human. It will take several days, but that is a positive thing. If you became human all at once, the transition would be a bit jarring, to say the least. After all, becoming human is not easy, nor is becoming a Sleepbringer."

"Yes, I understand." I smile. "If anything is troubling me, it is that I will miss you."

"I'll still see you. As before. In your dreams." She blushes, and a slow smile spreads over her lips. "The elders and I will be sorry to see you go. You have served us quite well."

Chimere is never stingy with her compliments, so I note with some consternation that she says "quite well" instead of "superbly," or "outstandingly," or "without fail." That is the best I can hope for. Nearly a decade has passed, and yet one incident, one transgression, mars my record with Chimere. Originals have never been human, so Chimere doesn't understand that if given the same chance, I would do things much the same. I suppose if a thousand years passed, she would still not forget it and still not understand.

She scans the street. Most of the lights in the houses along Peasant Street are still ablaze, but I do have my three other charges to tend to. She must be thinking the same thing, because she says, "I know it's a lovely night, but are you going to stay out here until dawn?"

"I can't very well move on if I'm talking to you," I say with a grin.

She huffs dramatically and throws her parasol over her shoulder. A parasol that, since it's nighttime, is completely absurd. "Fine, fine." She bats her eyelashes for dramatic effect and disappears into the night.

I turn back to the window. Yes, it is time to move on. But for some reason, I am frozen in place.

It's just my nerves getting the best of me. Soon I will be alone in a new world.

Chimere's words, "Julia's beloved," repeat in my head. There are so many human concepts I know nothing of, things I've waited a hundred years to experience. Things I intend to experience.

A breeze gently blows through the tree, rustling the leaves all around me. Julia is still, and my next charge is waiting.

CHAPTER 3
Julia

My dad throws the car into park but keeps it running. "I don't think I can get any closer."

The street is filled with the cars of mourners, all here to say a final farewell to my boyfriend, so yes, I guess this is it. The end of the line. Time for me to face the music. For some reason, my mind is allowing me to think only in clichés. My eyes trail down to where I'm digging my fingernails into the vinyl armrest. I quickly remove my hand, but by then there are three little slits there, as well as the sweaty imprint of my palm. "Uh, I know. I'm going."

But my body refuses to move. I'm frozen.

My dad reaches over and pushes a lock of hair behind my ear, but I shake it loose so it falls back against my cheek. "Take your time," he says.

That's something my parents are always telling

me. They never push me. I could be spending this morning in bed, and they wouldn't mind. In fact, they would be perfectly happy if I stayed with them until I was sixty. As I'm starting to wonder why I'm putting this pressure on myself, why I don't just have my dad turn the car around and take me home, I remember.

It's Griffin. My boyfriend.

I can't let him down by not showing up, especially after making such a mockery of his death on the front page of the newspaper. That was just brilliance, Julia. Pure brilliance, I think.

I give my dad a peck on the cheek and push open the car door. The smell of grass greets me, and the heat burns my face. I totter among the headstones, heels digging into the mud as I make my way to the crowd of people gathered around Griffin's coffin. I can already hear the sobs of my female classmates as they huddle together, clutching tissues and talking about the "senseless tragedy." I can't help wondering, Do tragedies *ever* make sense?

One of the girls looks up and studies me with her red-rimmed eyes, then taps her friend on the shoulder and whispers. They turn to watch me, and it's almost as if big question marks are hanging over their heads in cartoon bubbles.

I know that the chasm separating Julia Devine from her classmates is as wide as it will ever be, thanks to that latest newspaper story. When my classmates get into the newspaper, it's usually in the Community News section. They get positive little puff pieces about awards won or scholarships received. Both times I've been in the newspaper, the first when I was seven, it was front-page news. The kind of news people whisper about, and not in a good way, so that all you want to do is close your curtains and hide under your bed. The kind of news you wish you could run away from.

Before, they eyed Front-Page Julia with pity laced with fascination. Now there's a little shock woven in there as well, as if I've finally proven them right and lost my marbles. If I could, I'd tell them, *I thought it was a joke! You would have thought so, too, if your boyfriend was as sick in the head as Griffin Colburn.*

The "dearly departed" was always prank-calling me, pretending to be the committee choosing runners for next year's Olympics, or the selections board at Rutgers, offering me a full scholarship if I'd participate in their clam-baking team, or the Italian American Society, insisting I had won a Lamborghini. I only did what any of them would have done.

The reporter from the *Courier Times* had the sense not to print the stuff about Griffin's fungus and his smell. Thank goodness for small miracles. But he did insinuate that I thought Griffin Colburn was a loose cannon. What the article said was "The victim's girlfriend, Julia Devine, believes that the victim's reckless nature may have contributed to the accident. 'He was always taking chances,' she said. 'Clearly he is responsible.' "

The weird thing is that his mom *still* asked me to give his eulogy. She probably did it before she saw the story alerting the world to her son's rep as an eff-up. At the time, she hugged me so tightly my gallbladder nearly caught in my throat, and moaned something about how she'd never be able to make it through the ceremony. Now I'm afraid that when she sees me, she'll want to squeeze the rest of my organs out of my body, on purpose this time. I'm behind a bunch of freakishly tall men in suits (did Griffin know a lot of NBA players?), but between them I steal a glimpse of her—skin white, body crumpled, looking like she's ready to jump on the coffin and join her son in the afterlife.

I can't really blame her; Griffin was her only son. Though she, of all people, should realize that wherever Griffin is, he's probably looking for the nacho dip and calling every last one of these mourners a pathetic sap. I can just hear his voice now: *Go home, Griffin Groupies. Take your Prozac.*

As I hide in the crowd, grimacing at the mud caked on my one good pair of heels and cursing the god who made it improper to wear flip-flops to these things, I hear a few voices mutter "eulogy." People in the crowd start to look at one another, confused. Because of the wall of guys in front of me, I'm not sure what's going on until I hear a full sentence: "Who is giving the eulogy? Please step forward." It appears that Mrs. Colburn has gone mute, or else has forgotten that she asked me, or else is picturing how she might slay me, because she's staring at the coffin as if attempting to levitate it.

"Here I am!" I say, squeezing past the Michael Jordan wannabes, waving a crinkled sheet of paper in my hand. My voice comes out wrong, too cheery for a funeral. Everything about me is wrong lately. I really should have listened to that little voice inside telling me to stay in bed. I turn the volume knob down and mumble, more weakly, "Um, here."

I wobble through the crowd, all eyes on me. My heels kick up the mud, and I feel it splattering on my bare ankles and the hem of the only black skirt I had in my closet. When I get to the podium, I attempt to look up, but all I see is Mrs. Colburn squinting at me like *How can you betray my son's memory?* and a bunch of girls hunched over, whispering and crying, crying and whispering. Crying for Griffin. Whispering about me.

I reach up and pat my cheeks; they're hot but completely dry. In a way, it's my fault that Griffin is dead; he died on the way home from my house at two in the morning. I should have seen how exhausted he was, made him stay, pumped coffee through his veins. But I didn't. Plus we were always together; he was my Pug (because like the dog, he made ugliness cute), number one on my speed dial. You'd think these things would bring about some emotion in me. Sophomores and juniors who Griffin barely spoke to in the hallway are wailing in grief right now, but me? I've got nothing.

I clear my throat. "Griffin Colburn was a good person," I say, pulling a lock of my hair forward to cover my right cheek, to hide the scars there, since I'm sure that's what everyone is seeing.

Shock, Julia, you're in shock, that's all, I tell myself. I mean, I'm not made of steel. If anything could make me cry, I'd think Griffin's death would be it. But that's not the type of relationship Griffin and I had. Where Griffin is concerned, tears are *not* an option. "He was a good friend to many."

I venture a peek over the podium, away from the weeping girls and Mrs. Colburn, and see Bret Anderson, Griffin's best friend, rolling his eyes. He pretends to string up a rope and hang himself.

Thanks, Bret. Love you, too. Okay, so it is cliché, but would they rather a dramatic reading of "Do Not Go Gentle into That Good Night"? I speak a little bit about how he'd gotten a full-ride academic scholarship to UCLA, how he was the "always smiling, happy-go-lucky, life-of-the-party" type of guy, and how he will surely be missed for many, many years to come. It's corny, but what else can I do? This is what I knew of Griffin. Even though we dated for almost a year, we didn't have deep, mind-blowing conversations. When we talked, it was mostly in the form of one-liners.

That's when the priest clears his throat. The wind whips my hair away from my face, and suddenly I feel the scars pulsating, screaming, *Hey, look at me!* so that it drowns out my voice. I cut the next full paragraph from my speech, quickly mumble a thank-you, and step away from the podium. After that, nobody makes eye contact with me, which, I've come to discover over the years, is much preferable to being stared down. I fidget about in my ruined heels, searching for a safe place to stand, but Bret, the only person I trust right now, is way over on the other side of the coffin.

The priest does the whole "ashes to ashes" thing and then people begin to walk away from the casket, milling about, looking lost. Tracy McLish walks toward me. We were best friends up until last year, when I was a freshman. She moved to town when I was eight, so she missed all my drama, and we became friends. The thing was, after the story broke, I still felt the same, but everyone else expected me to be emotionally scarred for life. She didn't expect that, so she treated me just like anyone else and made what was left of my childhood feel normal. But that was before I met Griffin. Tracy had a hard time "getting" Bret and Griffin; a lot of people do. Thin-skinned people need not apply. And Tracy, like most girls, is too easily offended. I know; I used to be that way, too. She started hanging out with us less and less, and I finally stopped calling her. It was just a mutual drifting-apart, I guess, so that's why I expect her to walk right past me. Instead, she stops and says, "I'm so sorry, Jules."

Her eyes are a little teary. Leave it to Tracy to get torn up over a guy she didn't even know that well. "Thanks," I say.

She hugs herself. "I just . . . wish everything wasn't a big joke to you. Like it was to Griffin."

"What do you mean? I'm just . . ." That's when I realize she must have read the newspaper article. But I know she means more than that. I haven't had a good cry since . . . well, since I started going out with Griffin.

She shrugs. "Take care of yourself."

I start to thank her, but by then she's disappeared into the group. Yeah, having Griffin as a boyfriend helped me develop a thick skin. I had to, to last even a day with him. Instead of greeting me with a kiss, he'd squeeze my ass and say, "What's up, Bubble Butt?" Told me I ran "like a Muppet" at cross-country practice. Said I should "suck it up" when my cat Banshee died. He called things the way he saw them, even if it sometimes hurt people's feelings. But that was just his way, and the price you paid for having a guy who was an utter blast to be around. The way he told stories, the way he lit up a room . . . he knew how to keep things light, fun. I was the only one who learned to take it *and* dish it right back at him until he thought of me as his equal. He was authentic, which is more than I can say for any of these people. Crying for a guy they hardly knew?

I look at the coffin and tell myself, That's Griffin in there. Your boyfriend. I cough and try to think of something that might make me cry, for Tracy's benefit. Three-legged puppies. Onions. That's all that comes to mind.

Nope, no tears.

I'm sure Griffin would be proud of me. But I can't help wondering if it means that I no longer have a soul. That maybe I am as messed up as people think I am.

CHAPTER 4
Eron

Mama's ancestors used to say, "A restless night is Satan on your shoulder." They had no idea that sometimes a lack of rest has more to do with the worries of the person seducing a human to sleep than the person attempting to sleep. Tonight, after I completed the seduction of Julia, my two other charges suffered terribly. I was late getting to them, because my mind was in a muddle. Evangeline, a lady who took a new lover almost every evening, couldn't seem to get comfortable, and Vicki, the sleepwalker, wouldn't stay in bed no matter how many times I guided her back there. I'd like to say that it was their fault, that *they* were the ones with too much on their minds, but I knew better.

That's not to say it isn't ever the human's fault. Sometimes I will stay at the bedside of one of my charges all night, and there will be nothing I can do. Humans worry. When I was a human, I barely ever slept after I met Gertie. Gertie could sing "Ave Maria"—or was it some other song?—like an angel. Chimere has always said that seducing me to sleep was her greatest challenge. I'd toss and turn and think of exactly what I would say when I finally did have the guts to approach Gertie. It ranged from direct ("You are so beautiful") to subtle ("You dropped your glove"), with a thousand other iterations in between. One time, I found her alone in the coatroom after church, and all I could muster was a subhuman grunt. Chimere used to tease me, saying I was the only charge she'd ever had who would get tongue-tied around women even in his dreams.

I've always taken great pride in my work with the seduction, because Chimere will tell you I possess a particular skill with it . . . however, my talents will likely get me nowhere as a human. Maybe I'm a much more adept Sandman than man. Still, I'm committed to not letting fear—or my inability to string two words together—stand in the way, not again.

Sleepbringers do not have homes, for we do not sleep, or eat, or enjoy time with our families, or do any of the other things that humans do in their houses. I spend a good portion of the daylight hours sitting in the trees outside the homes of my charges, alone, which leaves much time for thinking. That is all I can do, because straying too far from my charges is forbidden. After all, you never know when one of them might desire a catnap. Not that I mind; it is quite relaxing and I enjoy the solitude. At least alone I won't stumble over my words like a fool. My other two charges live by themselves, within a few blocks of Julia, and they never vacation or travel, so I am never able to explore fully how the world has changed since I left it. And because the Sleepbringers charged with lulling Julia's parents to sleep are solitary types themselves, I'm always by myself, save for a daily visit from Chimere. I know that things in the world have changed. The women I watch over wear tighter, almost obscene attire; their surroundings are far more opulent; they speak on telephones without cords and say things in odd ways. . . . And I thought they were a mystery before! I know that becoming part of this world will take some adjustment, but I'm hopeful that I've learned a thing or two from these hundred years.

Namely, not to hesitate to act.

It's usually pleasant sitting here, listening to the birds chatter and taking in the sun. But today I have far too much on my mind. I'm thinking about Julia's beloved, about the training.

At twilight, I'm checking my pocket watch when Chimere appears, right on schedule. She greets me with the customary "Hello, my pet." With her is a tall, brutish young man with straggly golden red hair that nearly covers his eyes. It's quite a mess, which makes me wonder if that is indeed the style these days. His unkempt hairstyle is in direct contradiction to his formal wear, a crisp black tuxedo. We Sleepbringers always dress in formal attire, though my top hat, overcoat, and pinstriped trousers are likely no longer in vogue. He, however, does not appear to be very comfortable in his stiff new suit; he's pulling on the collar and grimacing. His face is red. I think he is having a difficult time breathing. I can't help smiling; I felt the same way when they put me in my attire. It took years to grow accustomed to it. We never wore such finery at the textile mill, or anywhere else, for that matter.

Chimere smiles and instructs him to sit on a branch opposite me. When he does, the branch bows under his weight. We're probably the same height but he likely has fifty pounds on me. "This is Griffin Colburn, your replacement," she says to me. "Griffin, please meet Eron, who will be your instructor."

"How do you do?" I say, extending my hand. He grabs hold of it, crushing it between both of his, and gives it a shake that very nearly makes the whole tree vibrate.

"What's up?" he says, his tone brusque.

Chimere giggles. "I'm sure you two will get along splendidly. This is Eron's first time as a teacher but he is excellent at what he does."

I smile at her, basking in the compliment, only to notice that my replacement doesn't seem to be listening; he's focusing on his wrist, fiddling with his cuff link. He appears confused by it.

I try to envision this fellow holding Julia's hand, or simply standing beside her, but after a moment, I realize it's not possible. A few additional moments of silence pass, wherein Chimere and I study our newest recruit and then exchange a raised eyebrow or two. Finally, he gives up on his sleeve and nods, looking bored. "Cool."

Chimere clasps her hands together. "Well, then. I'll leave you to it." She gives Mr. Colburn a motherly pat on the arm. "Good luck. Please let me know if you need anything."

Approximately thirty seconds after Chimere disappears into the dusk, the uncomfortable silence ensues.

Luckily, he breaks it, by saying something to which I don't know how to respond. "Wow," he breathes. "Chimere is hot. Are all the girls here like that?"

He mispronounces her name, calls her something closer to "Chimney." I spend a few moments thinking about how to phrase my response. "She is not a girl."

"Well, I know. Whatever she is, she's smokin'. Are they all like that?"

Cool? Hot? Smoking? What are all these references to temperature? Baffled, I venture that he is stunned by Chimere's beauty, like I was when I first met her. "I don't know; I've never considered any others of our kind. This work is quite solitary."

He cocks his head. "For real?"

I nod and motion toward the window. It's dark. Julia has not yet returned home. "Chimere"—I pronounce her name carefully, Chi-*meer*, so that he'll get it right—"told me that you are Julia's beloved, yes?"

His eyes widen and then he dissolves into laughter.

Ah, perhaps it was all a misunderstanding. It didn't seem possible. I relax. "You are not?"

He runs his beefy hands through his hair and shakes his head. "You people are, like, totally unreal. The way you talk. It's just . . . priceless."

There's heat under my collar; this conversation is already proving tiresome. "How do you mean?"

"You sound like one of those old movies. Or my great-grandfather." He stops laughing when he sees the confusion on my face. "Sorry. It's been a really crazy few days."

I nod. I vaguely remember my first days as a Sandman, when everything was new. Things were odd, I suppose. Truthfully, though, I fit into this world rather easily—almost too easily. Chimere said I was a natural. Perhaps it was because I didn't fit so perfectly into the human world. I've always spoken and acted differently than humans, even when I was one.

"So yes," he finally answers, a hint of sarcasm in his voice. "I am Julia's 'beloved.' "

"Oh," I say, perhaps a bit more dejectedly than I'd planned. I motion to Julia's home. "So this must be familiar to you."

He shrugs. "The house, not the room. I've been to the house a couple of times." He moves closer to the window and strains to peer inside. "Julia wasn't the most . . . *physical* of girls, if you know what I mean."

I nod knowingly. Julia always seemed like a girl of great virtue.

He squints. "What year did you go toes up, again?"

"Nineteen ten," I answer.

"Holy mother, are you old. Back then girls got it on a lot earlier, didn't they? Wasn't the average life expectancy, like, thirty?"

I shake my head. He's making fun of me. I decide to change the subject. "Perhaps we should begin the training now. I have a lot to teach you."

"Okay, yeah. When do I get to do Julia?"

The words stick on my tongue like glue. "*Do* Julia?"

He leans forward, excited. "Yeah. Like, whatever. *Seduce* her." He makes an odd gesture with both hands, as if he's squeezing produce.

"Not tonight. I think it's best I teach you some fundamental rules before we get into that. You'll need practice before you actually carry out the seduction."

He blows a tuft of hair out of his eyes. "I know the rules. Chimere told me the basics. I want to get on with the show."

I draw in a breath and let it out slowly, then calmly say, "Mr. Colburn, I am sure that Chimere told you that if you're not fully capable of assuming my position, I will not be able to leave mine once my hundred years have expired. That means you have to be fully versed in everything we do, even if it requires hearing the same thing more than once. The curriculum has been established over the course of thousands of years and it's not my place to change it. I am sure you understand."

His mouth becomes a straight line and he crosses his arms in front of his chest. He doesn't understand, but at least he doesn't object.

"All right," I begin, "the most important rules to know are these. One: You are only in the humans' world to soothe them to sleep. You can offer certain protections, which I will explain in time, but they are limited. You must never put your own needs or desires ahead of those of your charges. Once they are resting comfortably, you must exit their locale. Is that clear?"

It appears his eyes have glazed over, but before I can wave a hand in front of his face, he nods. "Chimere told me this already," he mutters. "But fine, I get it. Just following the curriculum. It's your breath, not mine."

"It bears repeating," I return.

He nods. "Get them to sleep, and get out. Got it. Next?"

The days of training this boy seem to stretch out before me like a long, winding path. Perhaps this is the type of young man whom a young woman of today would be eager to call her beloved, but I can't imagine that dear, sweet Julia would lose her heart to him. If so, I am lost.

"Did Chimere teach you how to enter their bedrooms?" I ask.

He shakes his head. "No. How?"

I'm relieved when he leans forward, finally appearing interested in what I have to say. "You are completely invisible to humans. You are also able to pass quietly into their rooms without having to open windows, move furniture . . . All you must do is simply *think* you want to go through something, and you will."

"So we're like . . . ghosts?" he asks, turning toward Julia's window. The moonlight faithfully reflects our images. I look insignificant and mouselike next to his broad frame. "Phantasmic."

"Not at all. We don't haunt people. We help them," I say. I wonder if I will need to repeat everything more than twice. "And then we take our leave."

"Yeah, yeah, yeah. I told you, I get it, I get it. But you never just . . . I dunno. Peek in their underwear drawers?"

I give him a severe glance. "Surely not. You're not to disrupt their habitat in the least."

He laughs. "Okay, okay. I was kidding. What else?"

I take a breath. The next rule, I know, is going to be the hardest one for someone like this boy to comprehend. I can already tell that he is the type who isn't used to walking into a room unnoticed. This is a dangerous quality for a Sandman to possess, and though they all eventually learn their purpose, it's never without its struggles.

"The next rule is: You are not alive anymore. You are not one of them. The sooner you realize that, the easier this is going to be."

CHAPTER 5
Julia

I pop the tab on a can of Red Bull and take a long swig. Coming to track practice today was obviously a mistake. Everyone must expect me to be in mourning, because I am having major flashbacks to when I was seven. My teammates keep acting like I'm the one who died and I just happened to rise from my grave. *Dr. Phil says that everyone expresses grief in their own way,* I want to tell them. *I am perfectly normal!*

The way I express *my* grief, apparently, is by running a personal record in the mile. Instead of cheering for me, though, my teammates just gaped like I'd run on air. They seem to think that even if I'm not a blubbery mess, I should at least play the part.

"You kicked ass out there, Ippie," a voice drawls, and I know it's Bret before I turn around. He's on the track team, too, and the only one who calls me Ippie, which was once I.P., or Ice Princess. It's a nickname I'm proud of, earned because he and Griffin knew I was the only one who could beat them in an insult-throwing match. I turn to see him lounging on the grass, iPod buds in his ears, his trusty unsolved Rubik's Cube in his hands. Nearly three months ago he had this grand idea that he was so brilliant he could be like the guy in *The Pursuit of Happyness* and conquer the puzzle in two minutes flat. We're still waiting for him to discover the secret. I can't help thinking of the day Griffin stole it from him and solved it for him. Maybe not in two minutes, but he solved it. Griffin might have been a jokester, but he was also a genius, which was why teachers loved him, as exasperating as he was. "Was that a personal record?"

I collapse next to him. "Yeah. I feel really good today. It's weird. My lungs usually start to burn during that last lap, but I felt fine."

He sits up, throws the cube on the ground, and pops the buds out of his ears. "Interesting how your boyfriend's death seems to agree with you."

"It does not," I insist, though I was thinking the same thing. A familiar feeling rushes over me: the desire to punch him. If there's anyone I fought with more than Griffin, it's his best friend. Bret has always had it in for me. Together, the two of them were like machine guns, constantly firing at me. "When have you ever known me to get all teary-eyed?"

"True," he says. He doesn't realize that before I met him and Griffin, teary-eyed was my way of life. I was a wuss. But most other people could cry and it wouldn't mean anything; when I cried, it turned heads. "Though you did seem a little rattled yesterday. Or do you normally suck that bad at giving eulogies?"

Before I started dating Griffin, I'd have been insulted. But with Bret and Griffin, you learned to ignore the digs. They'd made me strong. They'd made the rest of the school see me as normal. Sure, Griffin had his sweet moments, but they were few and far between and always buried under sarcasm and practical jokes. I liked that. Maybe normal friends would sit around crying and trading Griffin Colburn stories until the end of the world, but not Bret and me. We're light; we float; we don't dwell on the depressing stuff. Not when there's so much room for humor in the world. "If you were up there, all you would have done was tell fart jokes."

He nods. "Well, yeah. Did you see the place? It was like a funeral."

"But what about you?" I ask him. "Why aren't you at home right now, crying into your pillow?"

I know the answer already. It's almost as if the smirk is glued to Bret's face, because it never goes away, not ever. He's like the Joker. Griffin and Bret never once talked about what happened to me when I was a kid, even though I know that they, like the whole town, were aware of it. They just accepted it, moved on. Similarly, if Griffin's death had any impact on Bret, you'd never know it by looking at him. Considering they'd been best friends since forever, most people would think that's kind of demented. And Griffin was more than Bret's best friend; he was his master. Bret was Griffin's little protégé; Griffin was the person he aspired to be. As I'm wondering how he can function without his fearless leader, his grin broadens. "I'm saving my tears for the candlelight vigil."

"Okay, well . . . just remember: I get to lead the group in

'Kumbaya' this time. You did it during the Heath Ledger memorial."

He leans back and yawns. I get the feeling he's trying to suppress a snicker. "All right." There's an unspoken rule to our sparring matches that if the other person laughs, he loses. Secondly, if you take too long to respond, you're toast. I start counting the seconds, one . . . two . . . But he finally says, "You always did have a way with 'Kumbaya.' The smooth vocal stylings of Ippie Devine. Maybe you can delight us with 'Thriller' as an encore?"

I turn to him, speechless, and then say, "Well, maybe you can sing . . . uh . . ." But I can't think of a comeback. Three: if your comeback is pathetic, game over. Though I'm able to win sometimes, he's usually the victor. Griffin was the undisputed champ, but Bret's more of a natural at this than I am.

"Bzzzz. Thank you for playing. This game called on account of lameness," he says proudly, pushing on an imaginary game-show buzzer with the heel of his hand.

Just then a couple of senior girls, who I'd seen at some of Griffin's parties, walk by. They raise their eyebrows at us and start to whisper. "They think we should be wearing black, I think," I say, nudging him.

He starts to stretch his quads. "Black really doesn't do anything for my complexion."

I've known Bret for a year and not once has he ever expressed any remorse for acting the way he does. He's Griffin's smaller, lighter twin—and he may even be a little cuter, too, except he isn't half as outgoing as Griffin was. He was Griffin's comedic sidekick; it was almost like he enjoyed being in Griffin's shadow, following in his footsteps, being the butt of his jokes. And really, as both of us could attest, being known as Griffin's shadow was way better than being known for other reasons. I say, "And my black singlet is at the dry cleaner's."

Coach calls the guys to run the 400 m, which is Bret's specialty. He gets to his feet, then throws an arm around me and pulls me close to him. I can smell the cinnamon Mentos he's constantly popping. He lays a few good noogies on me and says, "Guess it's just you and me against the world."

It's uncomfortable being so close to him. I pull away and straighten. "And Satan," I say. "Don't forget Satan."

The joke doesn't hide my discomfort. He tries to position himself closer to me again, but I take a step back. Finally, he nods, a rare thoughtful look on his face. The smile is still there, but his expression is just . . . changed. It's scary, because I'm not used to it. "How can we forget Satan?"

The coach calls for the runners to line up, and he just stands there, oblivious. I point toward the track. "Go get 'em."

His face returns to normal and he gives me a thumbs-up. "Consider 'em got," he says, jogging away.

Off in the distance, a gaggle of girls is stretching on the green, whispering. Every so often, one turns and looks at me. It hardly seems fair. I've barely been able to shake the stigma from the last incident, and now here I am again, Front-Page Julia, the dead guy's girlfriend, propped up in the spotlight for all the world to examine like some sad sideshow act.

CHAPTER 6
Eron

In all my years of the seduction, I have never felt so uneasy. Last night was a lesson in frustration. Everything I explained to the boy was greeted with "But why?" or a snide remark. If he had been one of Mama's stepchildren, she would have already taken a belt to his rear countless times. Tonight I expect much of the same torture, but worse. Tonight the agenda calls for me to introduce him to every one of our charges.

I bring him to Evangeline's window first. He follows me with a decidedly human masculine swagger, and I wonder if he will ever assume the graceful floating typical of our people. Evangeline is what many would call an attractive woman, though she is a bit too modern for my taste. It is obvious that Mr. Colburn finds her appealing, as he leers at her with human longing while she changes into her satin negligee.

I'm ashamed for him. "You might show some respect and avert your eyes," I suggest.

He looks at me as though I've grown another head. "Why? She can't see me."

"Even so . . . ," I begin, but realize it's pointless to argue.

I try to convince myself that in another few weeks it won't be my concern.

"Whoa. She has some rack," he says with a grin. "So, she's the slut?"

I bite my tongue. I never said that. I simply said that she wasn't one to sleep in her own bed. Most nights, I'd have to track her down in one strange bedroom or another. Silliness; one would think that by now she'd realize that I do my best work in a familiar bedroom. But I suppose he's right; many humans do not hold their slumber as sacred as we Sleep-bringers do, and Evangeline is one of them. She prefers to dabble in other, less healthful pursuits. As much as I hate to agree with him, she is a woman with loose morals.

She slides into bed next to her latest conquest. A slight man with dark, wiry hair wraps his arms around her as the sheet falls over them. Then she reaches up and turns out the light on her night table. I turn to the boy and say, "This is where we come in." I move toward the window, and he stops me.

"Whoa, whoa, whoa. How do you know they're not going to get it on?"

"Get it . . . ?" I begin, but then shake my head. Another vile new turn of phrase I'll need to learn before I become human. "You will learn to know your charges intimately. She is clearly tired and ready for me." He moves to follow me, so I quickly hold my hand out. "Stay here. Watch this one from outside."

He narrows his eyes, but I ignore him. I suppose I could have him follow me, as it's not as if Evangeline can see us, but I simply must have a few minutes' peace. I pass quietly into the room and stop at her bedside. One foot, toenails painted red, is peeking from beneath the sheet. This is her usual way of sleeping. Leaning over, I whisper sweet nothings into her ear, then take the sand from my pocket and sprinkle it on her head. I begin to run my hand along her body, over the curves but never touching them. Her heavily lashed eyes flutter and then go still. In another moment, she is asleep, dreaming of the farm where she grew up. I rise and quickly pass through the window.

"See how simple it can—" I begin, but then I hear a girlish giggle coming from the branches above. Mr. Colburn is leaning against a tree limb, facing completely away from the window. He's smiling up at a young woman I've never seen before. She is wearing a long, formal dress and is enraptured by my student. She's obviously one of our people. "Mr. Colburn, have you been watching?"

He looks at me lazily. "Sorry, I'll catch the next one. This lovely woman—" He turns to her. "What did you say your name was, again?"

She blushes. "Genevieve."

"Genevieve was just telling me a great story about a dude who fell asleep at dinner and ended up with a beard of spaghetti," he says, and then a short laugh that sounds a bit like the honk of a goose erupts from his throat. "You guys know how to live it up."

I glare at the girl. Seducing someone to sleep when they're clearly not ready is strictly forbidden; however, sometimes it is necessary when a charge ignores the call of exhaustion for too long. Still, this unpleasant task is not something to brag of, and certainly not something to laugh about. "What are you doing here? Where are your charges?"

She points at the window. "That man — Bruno — is mine."

I nod and say as pleasantly as I can, "Well, I have much to teach my trainee, as I'm sure you'll understand, so . . ."

She nods sadly, gives the boy a doe-eyed look, and disappears.

He grins. "Thought you said this was solitary work, old man."

"If you are doing it well, it *is* solitary work," I return, businesslike, drawing the chain of my pocket watch from my vest. I check it; it's after ten. "We'll need to get to Vicki soon. She'll be going to bed shortly. And you must be careful with her. You have to be sure she is deeply asleep. She tends to walk in her slumber."

He follows me down the street, to the wet grass outside Vicki's home. It's fortunate that she lives in a one-story house, as she often trips and bruises herself during her sleep-walks. Sometimes I can guide her back to bed, but other times she will swat me away. She's over fifty and has lived alone since she left her parents' home as a teenager; she is used to doing things her own way.

My student peeks through her window. Vicki is sitting up in bed, bifocals on, reading a book. A cigarette is burning in the ashtray at her bedside. In the light, her hair is the unnatural color of a vibrant sunset, and the shadows and smoke bury themselves in the wrinkles of her face, making her look older. "Holy mother . . . ," he breathes, then turns to me. "You're not serious."

"About?"

He points a thumb toward the window. "*That.* That broad is older than you are."

"And?" Clearly I no longer have the patience to reply in full sentences.

"And I'm not going to do a lady who's old enough to be my grandmother," he chokes out. "That's repulsive."

I sigh. "Mr. Colburn, you seem to think that you're having a romantic relationship with your charges, and that is not the case. You are simply soothing her to sleep." Vicki reaches over, lays her book on her bedside table, and turns off the lamp. I pass halfway through the window and realize he's not watching, again. He's concentrating on the busy street outside, where a trio of tan girls with white-blond hair is strolling and giggling. I snap my fingers at him. "Perhaps you'd better come with me."

"Yeah?"

"Close your eyes, imagine yourself weightless, sliding through the window as if it is air."

He does as he is told and follows me through, tentatively. One's first time can be a little frightening and thrilling, as the feeling of passing through solid matter tends to send shivers up and down the length of one's body, as if every inch of skin is alive. "Whoa," he whispers, blinking, when we're standing in Vicki's bedroom. "I need to try that again."

"Later," I say. "And you don't have to whisper. She cannot see or hear us unless she's asleep. And even then she'll think she's dreaming."

For the first time, he's silent. It's as if he enjoys doing the opposite of what I tell him. I pad on the lush shag carpeting to Vicki's flowered comforter and pull a handful of sand from the pocket of my jacket. "Take only a handful, no more." He watches as I sprinkle it over her and it dissipates in the moonlight, casting her skin in a powdery glow. I whisper sweet nothings again and begin to move my hand gently above her, a hair's distance away from her skin. "You see," I say to my student as I work, "I'm not touching her, not at all. Never touch them."

He leans in closely and observes. "No touching? What would happen if—"

I sigh. "Just don't."

Vicki always takes some time, shifting from her side to her back to her stomach before she finally relaxes enough to let me do my work. Fifteen minutes pass, and just when her breathing begins to slow and I think I've got her, she sneezes in my face, clutches her pillow, and flops over onto her side.

I wipe my face with a handkerchief. This is one of the less glamorous parts of the job.

"Well, this sure blows. Is there an upside to this job, then?" Mr. Colburn groans, studying the pictures on the top of her bureau. "Hey! She was kind of hot, about a thousand years ago. You might have even dated her, when you were alive."

I attempt to ignore him and continue my work.

"So, yeah, you never told me. How did you die?"

I hold up my hand to him, to say, "Stop."

"Just making conversation," he says from behind me. In Vicki's vanity mirror, I can see him reaching out to touch a glass figurine near the frames.

I quickly straighten and grab his thick wrist before he can come in contact with it. "*Don't* touch anything," I demand.

"Whoa, sorry, man," he says, putting his hands up in surrender. "I wasn't going to move it."

"Do you not remember the first rule I explained to you?

You carry out your work, and then you leave. You do not touch anything." I turn back to Vicki, who is now stirring again, thanks to Colburn's disruption. "It won't matter to Vicki if you speak, because she cannot hear you. But I can. And I do require silence for this part of the process."

He claps his heels together quickly, like a soldier, and salutes. *"Aye, aye, Captain!"* he shouts firmly.

Fortunately, he watches carefully and silently as I carry out the rest of the seduction. When Vicki is snoring, I turn to him.

And cringe.

He's holding Vicki's smoldering cigarette in his hand.

"What did I tell you?" I hiss, snatching it from him and depositing it in the ashtray near her bed.

He holds out his hands. "It . . . was going to fall into her bed. She would have burned alive, man."

I narrow my eyes. "So? Did I not just say that you do not touch anything? No exceptions."

"But Chimere told me that we protect them—"

"We offer *some* protection, but within limits. You do not touch them. You do not handle human objects." I see his puzzled expression and sigh. "For example, you may offer them advice in their dreams or comfort them while they sleep. As a human, do you not recall waking up from a good night's sleep and having the answer to a seemingly impossible problem that had been plaguing you the day before? Or feeling energized and relaxed after a particularly stressful day? That was the work of your Sleepbringer, Chimere.

"In this situation," I explain, "you could have warned Vicki in her dreams that danger was near, so that she would awaken and put out the cigarette herself. Do you understand?"

43

He doesn't speak, just lets out a grand puff of air that blows the mop of hair out of his eyes.

"All right," I say. "Julia's next. But I often come back to Vicki's home two or three times during the night, just to make sure she hasn't walked off."

He eyes the woman in disgust. "Wow. You should just let the old bag walk out into traffic."

I glare at him, hoping he's joking. He doesn't flinch under the weight of my stare, so I say, "That is not funny. Only an Original, like Chimere, is allowed to seduce a human to her death. You are, in essence, to care for your charges as you care for yourself. Protect them. You must never even talk—"

"Jeez. I was kidding," he groans. "You people need to lighten up."

"If Chimere hears you talking like that, she'll never let you assume this role."

He snorts. "There's a fate worse than death."

"There's worse. They can put you in the Last Place."

He laughs. "Are you telling me they rank us? If I come in last place, do I still get some lovely parting gifts?"

"The Last Place," I repeat. "It's like purgatory for the most depraved Sleepbringers, the ones who fail miserably at their duties. A prison."

He snorts. "I practically *owned* the detention room at school. I bet they already erected a memorial to me there."

"It's not something to laugh about. Every day there will seem like an eternity."

He smiles slyly, as if to say, *What would you know about it, old man?* Hopeless. I don't bother to continue my warning.

We step outside. "You'll come to realize that you crave the

seduction the way humans crave sleep. You won't be able to avoid it." In the moonlight, I study him. He does look rather haggard, his eyes sunken. "You'll need to seduce soon."

Somewhere in the garden, a cat meows. "I thought you said I had to wait. That I was too much of a newbie or something."

"You are, but you'll have no ability to concentrate on your studies unless your mind is sharp and clear. And for that, you'll need to perform a seduction."

His eyes brighten and he rocks back and forth on his branch. "Bam-chicka-bam-bam. Yeah, baby. Lead the way. You said Julia's next?"

"No, I never said you'd be seducing Julia," I say. At that moment, that cat appears, rounding the corner of Vicki's house. It's yellow and fat, and unlike a human, it can sense us. It purrs, warming to us immediately. Animals love us. I take it as serendipity that this feline is here at this exact time. "I said you'd have to perform a seduction, but you are too new to perform it on a human."

He studies me, then the cat, and his jaw locks. "No friggin' way."

"We cannot continue if you don't." I stroke the cat's soft fur. "And cats are easier. It's a nice starting point."

"I am not. Freaking. Getting with. A cat," he says, curling his lips in disgust.

"As I said, you are thinking about it like a human. Remember, you are no longer human."

He eyes the animal and frowns. I have to say, it's quite satisfying.

CHAPTER 7
Julia

Griffin was the only customer I ever had who ordered item number 1.26 on Sweetie Pi's menu. Number 1.26 is an egg cream, a drink made with chocolate syrup, milk, and seltzer. It is gross. I'm just thinking about how my egg cream–making skills will seriously suffer without him when a gaggle of senior girls line up outside the stand, studying the menu. They're all holding shopping bags from Forever 21 and Hollister and smacking their lips. Since I've worked at this stand in the food court since freshman year, pre-Griffin, I have a knack for predicting what certain customers will order.

Judging by their waistlines, I can tell that these girls are fat-free vanilla yogurt in a kiddie-size cake cone all the way.

Well, actually, I can't claim psychic powers; I've waited on these girls a zillion times. One, Kiki Nickelson, has been coming here just as long as, if not longer than, I've been working here. Considering how often I see her at the mall, her dad must be harboring some serious guilt issues over giving his daughter such a goofy name. He seems to have surrendered to her full control of the credit cards as a peace offering. She looks at me and says, "Oh, hey, Julia. What's up?"

The good thing about being Front-Page Julia is that people who would otherwise call me "hey, you" do know my name. The bad thing is that that's about all they care to know.

"Not much," I say, still sporting my "can I help you?" smile.

Kiki's face falls, and I can tell right away that she has made the connection between Griffin and me. Tears flood her eyes—real, honest-to-goodness tears. "Ohmigosh, I am so so so so so sorry about Griffin," she says, smacking her heart with her manicured hand.

"Thanks," I say. She and Griffin dated, many moons ago, until, as he put it, "I got so sick of her I had to Kiki her ass out the door." He said she was about as high maintenance as the space shuttle.

The other girls offer their condolences and put in their orders. I was wrong; they all order fat-free vanilla in kiddie cups instead of cones. When I hand over the goods, Kiki is still giving me the sad puppy eyes. "You look like you're holding up pretty well."

I nod. The biggest problem with tragedies is that afterward, the world expects those affected by them to cease all functioning. I think everyone was expecting me to be lying here, a mangled heap of body parts, like a Picasso painting.

"If you need anything, just let us know, okay, Jules?" another girl says, dropping a five-dollar bill into the little tips canister at checkout, then patting the top of it as if she's donating to the Dead Boyfriend Support League.

I smile, knowing that if I ever attempted to take them up on that offer, they'd run like hell in the other direction. My experience with tragedy is that people will offer condolences and support but never be around when you want to collect. That was the way it was when I was seven; I was utterly alone. Yeah, things were better when I started dating Griffin; it felt like I was making my way back to Normalsville after an extended absence. Being Griffin's girlfriend showed everyone I wasn't contagious, or a ticking time bomb ready to explode. That gave me confidence. I cringe, remembering how I'd get whenever someone ignored me, or gave me that mock-sympathetic look, or whispered behind my back, *There's that girl! You know, the one who . . .* I'd cry and get all flustered, which just kept the rumor mill churning out news of how Julia Devine would never, ever be normal again. *She's obviously still scarred,* they'd say. *Mentally unstable.*

Griffin's reputation also preceded him. I knew he'd had a long line of girlfriends, and every week, someone different was gossiping in the girls' locker room about how difficult he was. Most of the time, they would whine about how he never took anything in life seriously, which sounded just wonderful to me. Because if there was one thing I was sick of, it was people taking me so seriously. And then Kiki would say, "He called me higher maintenance than the space shuttle!" and Bad Breath Britney would say, "He told me that whenever I opened my mouth, it smelled like a raw-sewage plant." They were all so insulted, but the more I heard about him, the more I liked him. He was *right,* after all. He just called things as he saw them. They, maybe, were too sensitive to put up with it, but I knew that if I ever had the chance, I would handle it. I would force myself to.

And then, miracle of miracles, the chance came.

It was a Saturday, right after Thanksgiving, so the mall was packed solid. I was already a little frazzled, because one of the girls who usually worked with me had just quit, and I was stuck with a bunch of newbies who kept asking stupid questions like "What is the difference between sprinkles and jimmies?" The line for ice cream wrapped past the Sunglass Hut stand, it was the end of the day, and my feet were killing me. And then there he was, standing in front of me.

At first I didn't think I could speak, but I channeled my inner Avon lady, put on my plastic smile, and said, "How may I help you?"

He rubbed his stubbly chin and studied the menu. The first thing one noticed about Griffin was his thick mop of reddish blond hair, which always fell just a tiny bit below his eyebrows. When he looked up, his gorgeous eyes were visible; he had eyes that were round and big and blue, enough to make some babies jealous. And he was tall and broad and substantial; you couldn't help seeing him. At Sweetie Pi's, we pride ourselves on having "3.14 hundred menu items!" which customers order by the number. Griffin smiled slyly at me—his smiles were always laced with mischief—and said, "Do you know all these menu items by heart?"

Leave it to Griffin to have no concern at all about the several dozen people waiting in line behind him. I'd been working at Sweetie Pi's on Saturdays since the summer had ended, so although I wasn't the master of the Sweetie Pi's operations manual, I was pretty competent. But right then I didn't want to play games, even with Griffin. My smile dissolved. "Yep. What do you want?"

"Um, how is your three point one three?"

I pushed away from the counter. "Is that what you want?"

"Depends," he said. "Do you know what a three point one three is?"

"Of course," I said. "Is that what you want?"

He leaned over the counter, reached up, and covered my eyes. "Don't look. What is it?"

I squirmed away. "Apple pie sundae. Is that what you want?"

"Eh, on second thought, no. How about your one point one zero?"

I stared straight at him. "The chocolate brownie fudge bomb?"

He crossed his arms in front of him. "Point two nine."

"Vanilla custard shake," I replied, unblinking.

"Point eight six."

"Lemon cookie bar blast."

"One point one four."

"Funnel cake."

"Two point zero three."

"Blueberry ice cream and caramel sauce on a waffle."

He grinned. "Impressive," he said in his Darth Vader voice.

I couldn't help breaking into a smile, but then I caught sight of the next person in line, this old lady, looking like she was about to launch her boulder-sized purse over the counter at me. "Is that what you want?"

He shook his head. "Nah. I'll take a one point two six."

I swallowed. What was a 1.26, again? "Sure," I said, then furtively looked at the menu. Egg cream. What the hell was that? Did it involve raw eggs? I'd have to take out the Sweetie Pi's manual to figure out that one, and then my cover as Sweetie

Pi's Master would be blown. I quickly turned to the back of the kitchen, trying to look like I knew what I was doing, when I caught him smirking out of the corner of my eye. He was totally on to me. "Ah," he said. "You are not a Jedi yet."

The line was growing longer, and someone turned up the heat on my cheeks. But then I remembered who I was dealing with. Griffin Colburn's whole purpose on earth was to get a rise out of people and never let them live it down. I calmly walked to the back and consulted the manual, then retrieved the ingredients. I poured a bit of milk into the bottom of a Sweetie Pi's fountain-drink cup, then filled the cup to the top with seltzer and drizzled the chocolate syrup over the foam. When I handed it to him and he paid, I said, "Have a nice day, Darth," and smiled as big as I could.

When I got off work, two hours later, he was sitting outside, waiting. For me? I was glad it was dark, because I was positive I had a chocolate-sauce smudge on my nose and quite possibly a raspberry one. It was cold, so I pulled my jacket tighter over my Sweetie Pi's T-shirt and tried to walk past him. He stood up as I did and said, "Your name is Julia. You're a freshman, right?"

I turned to him, thinking, Oh my God! My vocal cords froze up. Luckily, my facial muscles were too damn tired and cold to react in surprise, so I must have looked noncommittal and bored, like *Yeah, and who the hell are you?*

"Do you speak anything other than the language of ice cream?" he finally asked.

I was thinking he would go into the whole thing that some insensitive jerks would approach me with: *You were that girl. The one from the papers. Right?* But he didn't, and he didn't look like he wanted to satisfy his morbid curiosity by getting the inside scoop on it. Still, I was suspicious, so I said, "Darth Vader?"

He laughed. "So, you going to the fair tomorrow?"

My mind kicked into overdrive. Fair . . . fair . . . fair. What fair? This was cruel and unusual punishment for a girl who had just worked a mind-numbing eight-hour shift at a restaurant that combined food and geometry.

"The Brighton Christmas Tree Fair?" he finally said.

"Oh. I don't know," I said, still frozen, because oh my God, was he asking me out?

"Julia," he said in his Darth Vader voice, "I am not your father. That means we can go to the Brighton fair together and nobody will look at us funny."

I couldn't help it: I burst out laughing. After that, I realized that if I ever wanted to look calm, cool, and collected, all I had to do was pretend to be bored and tired and just keep my mouth shut. Easy. It didn't matter what I was feeling on the inside; it was all about what I showed on the outside. From that day on, I was officially Griffin's shadow. We were always together. He hated it when I rolled my eyes and looked away, but he also couldn't get enough of it. Most girls would pout or complain . . . but I had found the thing that made him weakest—pretending not to care, even when I did. Griffin always spoke in slogans from television commercials, and one of his favorites was "Never let 'em see you sweat." After a little practice, I was a pro at that.

Now I pour some milk into a cup, squirt in some seltzer, and drizzle on some chocolate syrup, then take a sip. Still gross.

"You eating into the profits, Ippie?" a voice calls over the counter. "Mr. Pi would not be pleased."

I take another sip and roll my eyes. Bret works at Gyro Hut, across the food court, but the food there is borderline inedible. He's constantly coming over here to eat into Mr. Pi's profits. I scoop a cone full of rocky road, his favorite, and hand it to him. "Don't you have a lamb to slaughter or something?"

"Oh, my little *tzatziki*," he says, grinning. He usually uses the word *"tzatziki"* a hundred times in one conversation at the food court, because he likes it, which makes food court conversations with him especially annoying. "You know I don't slaughter lambs after noon."

"How can I forget?"

He stands there idly in his white paper hat and hummus-stained apron, reading the menu, I guess. It appears he has forgotten his ice cream, because chocolate trickles down his wrist, and he doesn't seem to care. I find myself wishing I had a customer, but the mall is pretty dead today. "So . . . what's up?" he finally says.

"Um . . . not much." Scintillating conversation. Only then does it strike me just how weird things are with Griffin gone. Like Griffin was the central link in the chain that held us all together.

"Ippie . . . you're like a ghost now." His voice is playful.

I stare at him as he licks the ice cream. "Huh?"

"Like, I rarely see you."

I have no idea what he's talking about. I saw him at school two days ago, and at the track meet yesterday, and here today. Does he want to hang with me when I use the bathroom, too? Okay, so our interactions have been kind of short compared to when Griffin was around and we'd spend hours at his house, goofing off. But Griffin is gone. And I can't say I've been pining for time with Bret the past few days. If I hung out that much with him, it would be like we were *together*. I'm about to make a remark like that when I see the way he's looking at me. It's not a normal Bret look. It takes me back to the track, when he pulled me so close I could feel his breath on my cheek and smell his cinnamon Mentos. It's a look that kind of makes me think "together" is exactly what he has in mind.

I put the egg cream down and grab the edge of the counter. Suddenly, I can't breathe. This creepy-crawly sensation finds its way to the back of my neck.

"We could, you know . . . ," he is saying. "Hang out together . . . later."

My mind screams, No! And suddenly I'm feeling hot. I'm not sure why. After Griffin, Bret is a natural choice to fill the void. He's cute. And we had Griffin in common. Who knows, two shadows together might even make one real person. He's the only person left in the world who treats me like Julia, not Front-Page Julia. But . . . "It's just too soon," I whisper, and it's the truth, even though it sounds so pathetically cliché. I know that my face is flushed, so I turn around and chant *You don't care* to myself until I feel it return to normal.

He backs away. "I didn't mean *that* kind of hanging out," he says, clearly confused by my reaction. After all, he's never seen the old, weepy Julia. "I meant, I dunno. Get together. Play some *tzatziki*. And not strip *tzatziki*, either. Purely grandmotherly *tzatziki*."

"Oh," I mumble, embarrassed. Luckily, a woman with two children steps up to the counter. I muster a smile. "I'll catch you later."

His voice turns playful again, and he's back to the regular

Bret. "Catch you later," he says, and turns toward Gyro Hut, lapping away at his rocky road.

I turn back to the whitewashed cabinets and the harsh fluorescent lighting, then take a long sip of my egg cream, even though the seltzer stings my tongue. Things might have been normal with Griffin, and they could be the same with Bret, but maybe there's more than one definition of "normal." Maybe that kind of normal is not the one I'm looking for anymore.

CHAPTER 8
Eron

The rain filters through the trees, weighing down the leaves, making my branch wet, but I cannot feel the dampness on my skin. Sandmen are not affected by the weather, or so Chimere tells me. Yet just as I did as a human, I find rainy days to be gloomy. So many years have passed since I would arrive at the mill looking like a drowned rat after trekking the four miles through the city of Newark, and no longer do I have to endure the water seeping through the soles of my well-worn shoes . . . yet there is still something utterly melancholy about gray skies and softly falling raindrops.

Or perhaps it is just that with the passing days, the weight on my mind grows heavier. Before, it was only the apprehension of once again being human. Of finding my unfinished business. Now I have even more worries to contend with.

"Oh, my pet," Chimere says softly. "You are a sight."

I don't realize until she appears that I've been chewing my bottom lip raw. "I have much to think about."

She nods. "The training has been difficult," she says. "But of anyone, I knew you would be the most patient."

Chimere always uses flattery to motivate us. "I seem to be losing my patience with him."

"Yes. He is the challenge, isn't he?" she says with a giddy, schoolgirl laugh. As if I should be roused by this. I know how she, above all, loves challenges, but I do not. "I must admit, he does fascinate me," she says. "You are still making progress, in spite of it all."

I give her a doubtful look. "It took me nearly all night to convince him to try the seduction on a cat. I'm not sure he will ever learn to put his charges, even Julia, ahead of himself. He's quite self-absorbed."

"Yes, I know. I've spoken to him about that. He should be more amenable now."

"He's bitter."

She laughs. "And you were not, when I stripped you of your human life?"

She does have a point. It can be difficult to comprehend. "Did you explain to him that if it weren't for you, he would still have died, and had no chance of resuming his life? It was his time, and nothing could change that. You selected him for a greater, more fulfilling purpose. Did you explain that you were his savior, not his murderer?"

"Of course, but in any case, all that he once knew is gone. Though he may not show it, I'm sure he is very distressed. And understandably so. You must be patient with him," she warns, fluffing the skirts of her gown. "Give him time to get with the program."

I squint at her. "Get with the program?"

She smiles. "That's one of Mr. Colburn's phrases. I quite like it."

I shudder; no doubt I'll need a dictionary when I rejoin the world. "When will my transition to human begin?"

"It will start when Griffin performs his first human seduction. The more comfortable he becomes in that role, the more human you will become. As I said, it will happen slowly."

I find my hands quivering. Yes, I knew this, but the full reality of it suddenly hits me.

Tomorrow, for just a few minutes, I will be something I haven't been in a hundred years.

Human.

It's after twilight. A branch bows and my student appears among the leaves, clearing his throat. The arrogance is gone from his face, and even if that is only a facade for Chimere's benefit, at least he is punctual. Chimere is right. I should be more understanding. "Are you ready, my friend?" I say to him as cordially as I can.

"Yeah, bring it," he answers, eyeing me suspiciously.

Chimere giggles; no doubt she will be telling all the Sandmen she commands to "bring it" for the foreseeable future. She smiles approval at me, then turns to the boy. "I will catch you later," she says to him, rather stiffly. Another Griffin Colburn term, I am sure. Then she fades.

"You two look like you're up to something, old man," he says when she is gone.

I shrug. "I realized I haven't been very civil to you. This must be difficult to adjust to."

He hitches a shoulder. "I'm rolling with it. But it *is* kind of like ordering the prime rib and getting a cheeseburger. I mean, I can't touch her. I can't talk to her. So what's the point?"

"If you truly care for Julia, you will learn to put her needs above your own. Being a Sleepbringer is truly a most selfless profession. Something you should be proud of."

He rolls his eyes; he doesn't share my sense of pride.

"And after a hundred years you may go back to your life and complete your unfini—"

"Unfinished business, got it. Whatever that means. By the time I get back there, everyone I know will be dead." He shakes his head. "What is your unfinished business?"

"I'm not sure," I say. "I'd had plans to go to college for architecture. My father died coming over to America, but he'd wanted me to have these opportunities he never had in Italy. And then I went and got myself killed. You asked me how before, and I didn't answer. It was an accident at the mill."

"For real? Bummer. Was it gruesome? Blood and body parts scattered everywhere?"

I shrug. I can't remember much from that day so long ago, besides the shock.

"Mine was. Like *Night of the Living Dead*." He beams, as if he's proud of this fact. "But I didn't have any plans for the future. The only thing I was into was . . . I dunno, enjoying life. I cruised. Had fun."

"But you *did* enjoy your life. And when you died, you had two choices—either leave it forever, or become a Sandman and return to it after a hundred years. You made the right decision, did you not?"

"Oh, hell yeah. Definitely. But . . . a hundred freaking years. Holy hell." He rakes his hands through his hair and sighs.

I motion to Julia's window. She's going to bed early tonight.

She's wearing my favorite simple loose white gown and looks beautiful; I have to hold myself back from going in there and conducting my business. It's no longer mine. "If you'd like, you may seduce Julia tonight," I say, somewhat saddened by the prospect.

His eyes fill with hunger. I knew he'd be eager, but I had no idea how eager. He practically pushes me aside and storms through the window, rubbing his hands together greedily. He stalks to her—he still hasn't gotten to floating yet—and I move to the other side of the bed. He takes a handful of sand from the pocket of his jacket and begins to spread it over her.

"Not too much, only a bit," I advise, clenching my teeth. "Or else she will sleep far too long."

He raises his eyes to me for a moment and then continues his work. Julia is lying on her stomach, which she does often, so I cannot see her face. I cannot tell if it's working. He puts his hand over her and begins to run it the length of her body. His fingers are like plump sausages and move awkwardly, which is probably why, after a half hour or so, she rolls onto her back and exhales, still awake. Poor Julia. His hands stop in place and begin to shake.

"Don't touch—"

"I know!" His voice is a frustrated whisper. He starts to move his hands again. I want to tell him, *Gently, gently,* but I know he'd meet any of my attempts to help with the same unpleasantness, so I bite my tongue.

Another fifteen minutes pass. It's excruciating. I am told there will come a day when, as a human, I won't put the needs and worries of these women before mine, but right now that seems utterly impossible.

She turns onto her side and then sits straight up in bed, checking the clock. I, too, check the clock; it's likely Vicki or Evangeline is waiting for us. When Julia looks around the room, Mr. Colburn jumps backward, then studies her. Waves a hand in front of her face. She doesn't flinch. He waves his hand again, more fiercely this time, then screams, "Hello!" loudly enough to rattle my bones. No response. He shakes his head. "Wow. She really can't see or hear me."

I motion with my chin. "Keep to your work."

He steps back, his face stone. Giving up. Clearly he isn't used to being ignored.

I move to the bed and begin to run a hand over her, and within minutes, she is asleep. "See?" I say. "You were almost there."

He glowers. "She really, *really* doesn't know I'm here."

"Yes, but she might dream of you," I offer as consolation, though I know that Julia's dreams have rarely, if ever, been of him. It's most always those magnificent buildings, their tops hiding amongst the clouds. "Would you like to see her dreams?"

He cocks his head. "I can do that?"

"Sometimes. Just close your eyes, and think of her sleeping there." He does as I tell him to, and I do the same. "Can you . . ."

He's silent for a moment. "Oh, yeah . . . cool. She's . . . at the food court. At Sweetie Pi's. That's where she works. She's making . . . ha. She's making an egg cream. This is her dream? Seriously?"

"Yes." I watch the scene as he narrates it. So that is her place of employment. In all those times of visiting that place in her dreams, I'd never realized that. As she fills a cup with seltzer, I see someone approach. At first I think it is Mr. Colburn, which startles me; I have not yet shown him how to insert himself into her dreams. But then I realize it is another young man.

"What the—" Mr. Colburn breathes. "What the hell is *he* doing in Julia's dream?"

"Who is he?" I ask.

"My best—" he begins, his words clipped, but he stops midsentence as the young man drifts across the counter so that the space between him and Julia is nonexistent. His open mouth meets hers. He kisses her so ravenously, pressing his body against her with such force, that I can barely watch. I feel my face growing hot for her and have to pull myself out of it when I feel the heat radiating off Julia's skin.

"No, Bret!" a voice mumbles. Julia's.

Mr. Colburn's eyes spring open. Julia turns to the other side, clutching her pillow, still sleeping, still unaware of our presence. "Julia . . . ," my student says, bowing low to her ear. "Julia!"

"She cannot hear you," I remind him. I'm glad I haven't yet told him he can speak to her in her dreams; from the look on his face, he is far too unstable.

His hands tremble. His voice is ragged. "Why? Why was he in her dream? Why was he kissing her?"

I give him a smile to cut the tension. "When was the last time you were able to control what you dreamt of? It means nothing."

He processes that for a moment and then rubs his eyes. "It's got to mean something."

"Trust me. It doesn't." I say this only to calm him; any fool who has ever had a dream knows that sometimes they *do* have meaning. But only Julia knows what exactly it means. Thank goodness, his face softens. I check the clock at her bedside. "And we must be going on to our other charges."

He slowly follows me out the window but then stops to watch Julia before he passes into the night. For the first time, that happy-go-lucky grin has been replaced by a troubled frown.

"What are you thinking?" I ask him.

He doesn't answer, but I know. I know he is wondering if joining the Sandmen was the right decision after all.

CHAPTER 9
Julia

"How you holding up, Jules?" my locker neighbor Ebony asks when I stop to throw my bag into my locker.

"Fine, thanks," I say. It's the same answer I've given to every one of the three dozen people who have asked me the same thing. Maybe I should come up with something wittier. After all, I know the drill: they don't really want to know the answer. If I said something else, their eyes would glaze over.

Monday morning, all eyes are still on me. People step aside in the hallway as I pass. The funeral was weeks ago. I wonder how long it will be before they stop thinking of me as Front-Page Julia and start thinking of me as Julia again. Maybe that won't ever happen; after all, I was known as the victim for years after that incident when I was seven. That is, until I met Griffin. I remember the first time he kissed me. He stroked my cheek, right by the scars, and his hand felt like sandpaper. I shuddered. "I bet you're wondering how I got those, huh?" I whispered to him.

He grinned and whispered back, "Nope. I'm wondering why someone so smoking hot would be so stupid as to care about something so small. You need to keep your hair out of your face." From then on, he was constantly pushing my hair behind my ear so that it wouldn't fall down over my cheeks. We never talked about my past. I find myself wishing that he were here again, just to tell me what I'm having a hard time remembering now. What was it he used to say? *It's all in the past. Leave it there.*

I wish everyone would follow Griffin's advice. It's the last week of the school year, so in another three days, I won't see most of these people for months. I wonder how much of my past can be erased in a little less than three months. Maybe by the time I come back, I can just be Julia again.

Yeah. Fat chance.

I wonder what I'll have to do this time to be thought of as normal again. Before, it was Griffin who made me normal. Now . . . maybe I need to attach myself to a new guy. And the logical choice is Bret. I think about last night's dream for the hundredth time this morning and shudder. Though my brain is telling me that makes sense, my heart seems to want to run in the other direction.

All the students are walking around with that extra spring in their steps that comes with knowing summer vacation is just around the corner. Grades are in, so teachers aren't really teaching, students aren't really learning, and most of the seniors are nowhere to be found. That means Bret is probably somewhere else.

Thank God.

I have no interest in seeing him; after all, I saw enough of him in my dream to last several lifetimes. And there was something else about that dream, something weird, that I can't put my finger on. . . .

I slam my locker door shut. Dreams are just dreams. I am not thinking about this right now.

Ebony smiles at me. "Are you going to Mike Nash's graduation party this Wednesday?"

She's the first person who hasn't run away as soon as the "How are you holding up?" question was posed, who hasn't expected me to be in mourning for the remainder of my teenage years. "Um . . . well, I don't know."

"You should. You shouldn't just coop yourself up inside. It might lift your spirits." She studies me. "You look really beat, so getting out might do you some good."

I check my reflection in her locker mirror. She's right; I do. My cheeks look eggshell pale and my eyes are rimmed in red. "I didn't sleep well last night."

That's an understatement. I think I slept better the weeks after Griffin's death, which probably makes me evil and heartless, but it's true. Last night, it took me forever to get to sleep. Something was just not right—different, as if I were on new, scratchy sheets. Then, after that dream, I decided I didn't want to sleep. At all. Ever again. It wasn't just that Bret had his tongue down my throat, though just thinking about that now makes me tremble. There was something else really uncomfortable about the dream, but I can't remember what it was.

"A bunch of us are going, if you want to come along . . . ," she says, and I'm starting to think, Well, why the hell not? when I suddenly see him coming toward me in the busy hall. Oh, great.

Bret waves at me immediately, as if he's been searching for me. I feel my face getting hot. Ebony's standing next to me, oblivious to my meltdown, saying something about the party, but I'm completely lost. Especially when Bret stops at my locker and we're standing toes to toes.

It was just a dream. Get a grip, I think.

Still, I can't meet his eyes. "Hey there," I say as brightly as I can.

He leans his shoulder against the row of lockers. "Wow. You look like crud."

The image of our bodies pressed together pops into my head and I snarl at him, "You look like crap."

"Great, that was the effect I was going for."

Bret's grin turns wicked as his eyes fall on Ebony, like *Who are you and what are you doing with my property?* Despite the noise in the halls, an uncomfortable silence sets in.

Ebony narrows her eyes at him, then gives me a smile. "I forgot. If you go anywhere, I guess it would be with your *other* hip tumor." She motions in Bret's direction, slams her locker, and saunters away.

"No, wait—" I start, but Bret moves between us and laughs.

"So, crud-face, what's up?"

"Um, nothing," I say, suddenly wishing I were in bio. It says a lot when you'd rather be sitting in bio than talking with your friend. I watch Ebony head down the hall without looking back, and I hiss, "Do you think maybe . . . just maybe . . . I could have a conversation with someone other than you?"

67

It comes out meaner than I expected, and I immediately feel guilty.

"With who?" He tilts his head, then hitches a thumb in Ebony's direction. "With *her*? I don't even know who she is."

"So? I do. She's in my class. And we were talking about going to a graduation party on Wednesday."

His eyes narrow. "But you're not graduating."

"So?"

He puts an arm around my shoulder, and I nearly jump from the tingles it sends down my arms. "Okay, fine. If you want me to take you to a party, all you need to do is ask."

"I—I don't . . . ," I stammer, fists clenched. I don't want you, I think. Then I sigh. "I'm just . . . tired. I need to get to class."

"Let me walk you."

I shake my head. "No, I have two feet. They work, too."

"Oh, come on. Is it so bad that I want to make sure you're okay?"

"That's nice, but I'm fine."

"Right. You *say* you are. You're starting to do that girly, emotional, freak-out thing, and it's breaking my heart. I want the old Julia back."

"Maybe I don't want to be the old Julia anymore," I mutter. The old Julia would take the abuse and dish out some more. But lately I've just been too exhausted to even bother trying to be smooth and quick-witted around Bret, which reminds me how impossible that dream was. I expected that if I kissed a guy in a dream, it would be fairy tale–like, blissful. This was like kissing a Hoover. And it didn't help that Griffin was standing there, stone-faced, watching us the entire time.

Griffin.

Suddenly, it hits me. Griffin was in my dream. Had he ever been in one of my dreams before? No, not that I can remember. But now, *now that he's dead,* for the first time ever, I dreamt about him.

He was wearing a tuxedo, like he wore to prom. He was watching me, as if on the other side of a barrier he couldn't break through.

And he was not the happy, carefree Griffin.

Far from it.

The hallway seems to blur and spin, like I'm on a carousel. I look down at my hands. They're trembling. Bret must sense it, because he reaches out and steadies me with a firm hand on my shoulder. "Someone skipped breakfast," he jokes. But I am far from in a joking mood.

I take a breath. Dreams are just dreams.

Right?

CHAPTER 10
Eron

It's a beautiful, bright day and the shade of the oak I'm resting in feels heavenly. The windows are open in Julia's home and her pink lace curtains sway in the breeze, carrying her perfumed scent, like the smell of clean laundry, out to me. I smile to myself, thinking of wash day as a child, when my mother would hand me a basket of freshly laundered sheets to fold, and I would fall asleep in them, inhaling their sweet scent. I don't notice the absence of the incessant chirping of the birds that has always been my background noise until a grating voice nearly knocks me off my branch.

"What are you doing up there?"

I straighten and peer to the ground, between the branches, for the first time in a long while feeling rather dizzy. A bald man with a bulbous nose and ruddy cheeks is scowling at me. He's wearing a white T-shirt and gardening gloves. Again, I'm nearly knocked off my branch when a realization floods over me.

He can see me.

I quickly scramble down to the grass to meet him. When I

am on the ground, I stand a full head taller than he. "My good sir!" I say cordially, knowing full well how inappropriate a stranger hiding in Julia's tree must seem. I remove my hat and hold it in front of me. "Pleased to meet you. I am Eron DeMarchelle."

At that moment I note the large, rather threatening pruning shears in his hands. He jabs them at me. The scowl has deepened.

"And you are . . . ?" I prompt.

He takes a step backward. "Calling the police."

"No. No. No. You see . . ." I turn my hat in my hands. This is not how I expected my first day as a human to go. "I understand it may look strange . . . me in that tree . . . but I assure you, I was only . . ."

I swallow. What, exactly, was I doing?

He leans forward, squinting all the more, waiting for an explanation.

"I thought that perhaps my kite had flown into this tree."

The sharpness in his features doesn't diminish. "Kite?"

"Uh. Yes." I'm not sure where the excuse came from; I never owned a kite when I lived in the city, as many a child had lost them in the clotheslines. But did they not fly kites these days?

He looks up into the tree's branches. "Aren't you a little old to be flying kites?"

I smile sheepishly.

He points the shears at me menacingly. "You'd better get out of here. If I see you in this neighborhood again, I will call the police."

"Yes. Yes, sir," I say, heading across the lawn, toward the

street. If Chimere were watching, she'd giggle and say, *Making friends already, are we?*

When I am out of the view of the gardener, I marvel at the pavement, at the way the morning sun makes its surface glitter like a chest of jewels. It's been over a hundred years since I've been in a sun this brilliant; usually I'd spend the daylight hours hidden in the shade of the trees. In the dying orange rays of daytime, things take on a more somber, muted quality. Everything now is so much more intense I can't help blinking furiously.

A middle-aged man in shiny underpants lumbers toward me on the sidewalk. His face is ruddy, and he is breathing hard. His blank, unseeing eyes suddenly fix on me and narrow. It's been years since humans have looked at me, and I shiver from the thrill of it. I tip my hat and say, "Good morning," but the man does not reply. That is when I notice a small round device in his ear; the man must be hard of hearing. "Good morning!" I shout. But the man simply sneers and jogs on.

Chimere's voice rings in my ears. *Oh, yes. You fit in quite gloriously here.*

I shrug and continue down the path, squinting in the light. Everything—the rooftops of the neighborhood colonials, the leaves on the trees, the identical black mailboxes—everything glints as though it were winking at me, welcoming me. Or perhaps warning me.

I pull a crumpled paper from my vest pocket and study it, though I know perfectly well what it says: *V. Harmon, 26 Hart Avenue, 2B.* I memorized that information, for it holds the key to my human livelihood. How could I possibly survive more than a few days as a human without money, without a place to live? V. Harmon is a former Sandman who offered up a room and some other items to help get me on my feet. Though I've never met him, I know he will be welcoming; he received the same kindness from another former Sandman when he returned to human life. It will be nice to have one friend in this world, one understanding soul to confide in.

At the entrance to Julia's development, there are a few people standing at a small glass-enclosed shelter. It's a motley crew, a pretty woman with a baby, an old lady in a flowered dress, and a young man, perhaps my age, reading a magazine. The two women stare me up and down, looking shocked, and I'm certain it's because of my dress. A dark three-piece suit, a top hat, and spats are too formal and stuffy for such a warm day. Perhaps V. Harmon will have some more fashionable attire for me to wear.

I steal a look at the young man's wardrobe. A vulgar black cotton shirt, sleeveless, like underclothes. It says *Save the Trees—Eat a Beaver* on it. Blue jeans, the kind I wore in the factory. The young man doesn't look up. He slouches forward, rocking his head back and forth to some inaudible rhythm, a black nest of hair cluttering up his face. He, too, has wires coming from his ears; it's strange how so many young people these days have hearing problems. I lean over to him and enunciate, "Good day. Would you happen to know where 26 Hart Avenue, 2B, might be?"

The man turns to me. "Up yours, homo."

The lady with the baby taps me on the shoulder. "It's about ten blocks down that way," she says tentatively, inspecting me as she points down the street. Just then a frightening sight—a huge, hulking metal monster—screeches to a halt before me. I jump back, but the woman motions to it as two doors groan open. "This bus stops there."

"Thank you, ma'am," I say, tipping my hat. I marvel for a moment at the enormous vehicle. Of course. A bus! I've been on a bus only once, on a trip to New York City with Mama and my stepfather to visit some DeMarchelle relatives. This isn't the least bit similar. I offer my arm to the kind young woman, but she must not notice, for she struggles to step up on her own, hefting the baby on her hip with one hand and grabbing the handle with the other. The old woman swats my hand away and grumbles something unintelligible. The young man laughs coolly and steps inside.

I step into the well, climb the stairs, and feel a hand land firmly on my chest. An old woman with a stony face is at the reins.

"Good day, ma'am," I say.

"Ticket?" she barks.

Instinctively, I reach into my pants pocket, where I always kept my money before, all the while knowing what I'll find there. Nothing. I haven't had any money in a hundred years.

The driver shakes her head and points out the door. She clears her throat. "No ticket, no ride."

Bowing my head in shame, I step from the bus and it immediately crawls away, leaving me in a swirl of heat and foul-smelling exhaust. Not to worry, I tell myself. This situation will soon be remedied when I meet with Mr. Harmon.

For the next hour, I wander in the direction the young lady pointed in, until I come to Hart. In the meantime I see many indications that this isn't the world I left. I've seen a few motorcars outside the homes of my charges, but I had no idea how omnipresent they were; they're simply everywhere. Most seem to be congregating around a sprawling building, bigger than a mountain, with *Walmart* emblazoned on its front. I pass several people, but they all ignore my greetings; I hope that they'll be more friendly to me when I'm wearing new clothes.

The homes are less well cared for on Hart; they're smaller and remind me of the row homes from my old neighborhood. In comparison, the houses in Julia's area are castles. Perhaps I'll fit in better here, I think as I walk along the cracked sidewalk to number twenty-six, a small duplex with a crumbling brick facade. I climb the worn steps. There are four doorbells on the front, between two doors. I press the one that says *2B*. After a moment with no answer, I buzz it again.

I wait for at least five minutes, buzzing intermittently. I wouldn't normally linger so long. A few times, I turn back to the street, ready to leave, but then I realize there is nowhere to go. The thought makes me shiver, even in the sun.

I'm relieved to see movement behind the dingy once-white lace curtains on the windows. I remove my hat and say, "Good morning," as the door opens, but my voice falters when I see the individual behind the torn screen door. He's a younger man than I expected, perhaps thirty, and he's unshaven and wearing a partially open bathrobe, even though it's after eleven on a weekday. His eyes are bleary, covered by a mass of black hair, and he's holding a lit cigarette, the smoke from which billows out to meet me. Surely there is some mistake. "Mr. Harmon?" I ask.

He stares at me, his heavy eyelids drooping over his

unfeeling eyes. I know that look; I saw it on my stepfather more times than I can count. Drunk. At eleven in the morning. Disgusting. Shades of that cramped one-bedroom apartment above the deli in Newark crowd in. Combined with the foul smoky air, the effect is quite smothering. When he opens his mouth, I almost expect him to sound like my stepfather. But his voice is his own, not as raspy, higher-pitched. "You're that fellow."

It's not exactly unfriendly; it's simply stated as fact. But I'm glad when he opens the screen door and lets me pass through. Inside, the smoke mingles with the thick stench of an animal and the salty smell of urine. A cockroach scurries into a crack in the wall behind Mr. Harmon's head. I swallow. "Yes, I'm—"

"I know who you are." His words slur together, but not nearly as much as I expect based on his ragged appearance. "I got the whole rundown."

He leads me up a narrow corridor to another door. Inside, the stench is more putrid than ever. We stand in a small living room with bare walls, threadbare carpet, and nothing more than a misshapen green sofa and a small—what did Chimere call that item? Ah, a television set. Julia has one in her room. This one seems a little worse for wear.

Mr. Harmon holds out his arm, as if presenting a lavish estate. "Welcome to paradise," he says, chewing on his cigarette.

"Indeed." I don't mean to say that aloud, so it comes out as a murmur as I inspect the place.

"You were expecting more?" he asks. Several more cockroaches scurry between his feet. His bathrobe isn't lush and roomy; it's thin and barely meets his knees, stretched like a baby blanket over an adult. He is wearing long white socks, and the hair on his calves is so thick it curls over them.

"No," I say. I suppose that from my attire he has no idea that I was raised in a very similar situation. Though Mama had kept the cockroaches to a minimum; I catch sight of a pile of dishes in the sink and note that Mr. Harmon appears to be breeding them. "This will be sufficient. Thank you."

"There's only one bedroom. You can sleep on the couch," he says, waving his hand at the small misshapen green thing across the room. "When you get back to sleeping, that is. I didn't for a while."

"That's fine," I say. I lift the lapels of my jacket. "Do you happen to have any—"

He shakes his head. "Nah. I mean, I got a couple of T-shirts you can borrow. I'm not exactly well-off, you know."

He disappears for a moment and I hear things crashing around, drawers opening and slamming shut. He returns and tosses me a few yellowed, wrinkled rags that I suppose are shirts. I hand them back to him. "I . . . I think I will manage with what I have."

He shrugs.

"Sir," I begin, as gently as possible, "I was told that you'd volunteered to take me in because you—"

I stop when he laughs long and hard, spattering a bit of black smoke-laced spittle in my face. "Volunteered? Like I volunteered to join the Sandmen a hundred and fifteen years ago? Right."

"I'm sorry. I must have been mistaken."

"Yeah," he says bitterly. "So once I get done babysitting

you, my debt to them will be fulfilled and I can go on with my life . . . or death." He snorts. "Depending on how you look at it."

I fidget for a moment, unsure of what to say. There are questions I want to ask, but they all seem improper now.

Without a word, he slips into the kitchen and opens the door to his icebox. "You want a beer?"

"No, thank you."

"You sure? It'll help you sleep." He comes back with a bottle, takes a long swig, and jabs a finger at me. "You're fading."

I look down. My hand has taken on a ghostlike quality; I can see the floor through it. "What . . . ?"

"Always happens a couple minutes before you go back. You know, to the *other side.*" He lifts a hand and wiggles his fingers dramatically, then sniffs and wipes his nose on the sleeve of his robe. "Have a lovely trip."

The next thing I know, everything fades to blackness. When the light dawns again, I'm back in Julia's tree. The sun is strong, filtering through the leaves above me. Chimere is smiling at me, batting her eyelashes. "Was that first taste of human life everything you remembered?"

I stretch out on the branch, my body relaxing among these more comfortable surroundings. "It will take some getting used to."

"Oh, of course. But right now," she sighs, "I need you to attend to your student."

I study her face. It's quite serious. "Is something wrong?"

"Perhaps. Considering we don't know where he is."

CHAPTER 11
Julia

At the end of last period, I throw my books into my locker and linger there, hoping Ebony will come by and we can resume the conversation about the party without the presence of my hip tumor. I spend enough time there to begin growing roots, which is moronic, considering school is out and most students wouldn't spend another second here than is absolutely necessary. And I have the late-afternoon shift at Sweetie Pi's. Which means . . .

Ugh. Seeing the hip tumor.

I slowly turn and trudge to the doors, thinking, So what if I don't go with Ebony? I could go with him. He's one of my best friends. In fact, he *is* my best friend now. That wouldn't be so bad.

I cringe, remembering how things were when Griffin was alive. People knew me, yes. He might have made me appear normal, but Griffin and Bret were also like insulation. They made me feel safe, like part of the crowd. I didn't mind it much then. At least if I was with them, I wouldn't have to worry about being seen as the victim. I was just Julia. But now . . . now I can't stop thinking that as long as I'm with Bret, people will tie me to Griffin. I'll forever be the dead guy's girlfriend.

At the food court, I look toward Gyro Hut and see Bret's reddish hair peeking out from behind the pita-warmer. Quickly, I rush behind the counter, throw my stuff into my locker, and put on my apron. I'm not in the mood for dishing out soft serve today, especially since I know that Mondays are our slowest days and Bret will be over here just the second he sees my—

"Hey, *Tzatziki*!"

Kill me now.

I can't pretend I don't hear him. The mall today is quieter than a library, and he's shouting at earsplitting volume across the court. I turn, smile, and wave, then pretend to stack plastic cups into a model of the Empire State Building, working with great care and precision, as if this is something my manager asked me to do. As if the future of Sweetie Pi's depends on this statue. If I look like I am busy, he will leave me alone, right? No luck. He immediately jogs over to me.

"Not funny, not funny at all, Ipster," he says, wagging a finger at me like I'm a bad toddler.

This raises the question "What are you talking about?" but asking would require me to speak to him more, something I don't feel like doing. But he's not the type to go away if I play mute, either. "What are you talking about?" I finally say.

He reaches into his apron and pulls out his Rubik's Cube.

Well, it looks like his, but I can't be sure, because there's something very different about it.

It's completely solved.

"You did it," I say. "Congrats."

He gives me a tsk, tsk, tsk noise, still acting as if he's talking to a two-year-old. "You know I didn't."

I shrug. "You didn't?"

"Don't play dumb."

I glare at him. "I seem to think you were the one who told me that when it comes to dumb, I don't *have* to play."

"Touché," he says with a grin, pocketing the cube again. "But the fact still remains that you and Griffin were the only ones who had the combination to my locker. I left it in my locker over third period and when I got back, voilà."

"So wait . . . you think I broke into your locker?" As if I've wanted anything to do with him these past few days. And please, I wasn't the type to play practical jokes. That wasn't my thing.

But it *was* Griffin's.

"Don't give me that 'who, me?' look. It was you, wasn't it?"

The blood begins to drain from my face, but then I remember: this is Bret I'm dealing with. "Nice try. If you want to freak me out, you're going to have to do better than that."

He gives me the evil eye. I return it.

"Did you really expect to show me that and make me believe Griffin is back from the dead? You are lameness times a thousand. Go back to your *tzatziki*."

Bret doesn't move.

"Go away. You are annoying me," I finally say, turning back to my cups.

Bret's still standing there, frozen. The smile is still on his face, but it's a cautious one, as if he's wary about becoming the butt of someone's stupid gag and can't quite figure out how to respond. I know him well enough to know what that look means.

He's not joking. And if he's not joking . . .

And I'm not joking . . .

The only person left in this equation is . . .

Dead.

Which is impossible. So . . . right. It's got to be Bret. Bret playing a joke on me. That's the only logical answer.

"Go away," I say again, this time more forcefully. "Or I'll sic Griffin on you, since he's obviously back from the dead."

He laughs. "Fine. Gang up on me."

"I have work to do."

"Stacking cups?"

I sigh. "That's the thing with you and Griffin. You never knew when to quit. It's not funny anymore."

"Oh. But you're hilarious," he says playfully.

I slam a stack of cups down. "*Stop* it, okay?" I don't think I've ever raised my voice around him.

He takes a step back. The smile is still there, but only a hint of it. "You didn't go into my locker?"

I shake my head.

He shrugs. *"I don't believe you,"* he singsongs.

I throw up my hands. For a second, I think about telling him about my dream, not about the kiss, but about seeing Griffin there. But I don't. Dreams mean nothing. And this is Bret. If I told him that, he'd never let me live it down. My even entertaining the thought that Griffin is still here would give him enough material to make fun of me for the next hundred years.

"Fine, don't believe me. But maybe it's one of those little mysteries of life," I say.

He smirks, and I sigh, feeling like I just went fifteen rounds in a heavyweight title match. But hey, at least I survived, I think. Before Griffin, the first punch would have been a total knockout.

Before Griffin, lots of things would have been a total knockout. I remember that a few months before Griffin died, I'd gotten a rejection to the summer session at the *Architectural Journal,* something I'd lusted after for a year. Normally, I would have cried my eyes out for a week. But when I started to have my breakdown, he pulled me into his arms and said, "So what if they don't want you? Screw 'em. You're better than all of them, anyway." I tried to whimper that he was wrong and that it was the end of the world, but he gave me his stoniest look and said, "Girl, I'm going to count to ten. And by the time I do, you'd better be over it."

That always worked with me. After all, I was the one wishing people would keep the past in the past. The best way to make sure that happened was just to throw it there, as far as you could, and never look back.

As Bret heads back to Gyro Hut, I know I'm being a jerk. But I can't help it. I can't help thinking that as much as I want someone to understand me, going that route with Bret is all wrong. I want someone else to talk to. Someone real. Ebony. Someone, *anyone* else. More than ever.

CHAPTER 12
Eron

A bit after dusk, my student launches himself through the leaves like an act in a talent show and skids onto the branch next to me. "What's up?" he asks nonchalantly, as if everything is perfectly normal.

But everything is not. Chimere and I have spent the last three hours fretting over this.

"I believe I did tell you," I say, trying to keep my voice even, "that we frown upon your venturing away from the homes of your charges?"

He nods and grins. "Yep. I figured you were doing a lot of frowning upon me today."

"This is not some game. These humans rely on you."

He laughs. "That's just what Chimere said."

"Mr. Colburn, your indifference is not—"

"Look, old man, give it up. There was something I needed to do. And now it's done. And the world is not exploding. So stop giving me grief."

I glare at him. "Something you needed to do? What could you possibly . . ." It dawns on me at that moment. "There is nothing you could have needed to do outside the realm of your charges. The only thing you need to do right now is take care of them. Do you understand? *You are no longer human.*"

"Ha! That's what Chimere said, too. You guys must share a brain."

I rub my face with both hands, exasperated. "Please tell me that you did not touch anything in the human world to alert a human to your existence."

He makes a gesture with his thumb and index finger. "Just a little something."

I throw up my hands. "You are the most incorrigible soul—"

"Look," he says, his voice serious. It's startling how quickly his manner changes. "Julia is in trouble. I needed to help her."

I prick up my ears. Julia in trouble? "What kind of trouble?"

"That guy . . . the one she was getting with in her dream . . . He's making a move on her."

I sigh. Though the thought is quite discomforting to me, too, it isn't anything that we, as Sleepbringers, need to concern ourselves with. "And? Life goes on without you. You must let it."

He shakes his head. "He's not a good guy."

"I thought you said he was your best friend."

"Yeah, he is. That doesn't mean I trust him."

I suppose it's understandable that he would say these things; after all, he did witness a rather disturbing exchange between his beloved and his best friend, even if it was only in a dream. I recall my anguish at seeing Gertie in the arms of another man, so I can't blame him. As a Sleepbringer, though, he's likely to see Julia do many more things that he deems unwise, things he has no place interfering with. And yet the look on his face reflects mad, animal rage; he is clearly still thinking more like a human than a Sandman. "If your friend is 'not a good guy,' as you say, there is only so much you can do to protect her. I will show you how to speak to her in her dreams; you may be able to exert some influence over her that way. Touching anything in the human world is strictly forbidden. Much more of that will land you in the Last Place. And you do *not* want to be there."

He grinds his teeth into his bottom lip and exhales loudly. Then he reaches over and rips a branch from the tree. I bring up my hands to shield myself from it, in case he should throw it my way, but he doesn't; he simply tosses it onto the ground. "Can't suck any more than this does."

"We have to continue with your training," I say to him, checking my pocket watch. "Chimere would be—"

"Chimere can eat me," he snarls, then holds up his hands in surrender. "Fine. Fine. Let the learning commence."

"Don't say that about her," I say. "She was worried about you. She spent all day looking for you."

He clucks his tongue. "She had her head in the clouds, moping over you. That's why I was able to get away."

"Me?"

"She's got a thing for you."

I laugh. "A thing? You mean . . . No. That's not possible for Originals. We are very fond of each other, but that is all. Besides, I seem to recall her warming to you quite nicely."

"Yeah?"

"Yes. She seems to have adopted some of your colloquialisms, and I can't say she's ever done that before."

"Yeah, but whatever. You're, like, her perfect little protégé. I see the way she bats her eyelashes at you. And she talks about you like you're the man." He laughs. "Trust me. She's got a thing for you. And I'll never be able to live up to your saintly image. Tell me, have you *ever* done anything Chimere told you not to do?"

I'm about to tell him that he's wrong, so wrong, and what's more, that no female has ever had a "thing" for me, but I decide this is silliness. Besides, these topics are not worth discussing with the likes of him.

"Chimere is going to freak when you're gone, man. I'll be surprised if she doesn't beg you to stay."

"Chimere is not so silly," I say.

"People you know really well can surprise you."

"Chimere is not a person."

"Whatever. I mean, I was surprised by my best friend. Julia doesn't know him as well as I do. I've known him since we were kids. And I know now that he'll hurt her."

He'll hurt her. If any words could stop me in my tracks, they are those. I immediately think of my stepfather. Mama went to the grave two years after I did, thanks to him. If there was any day of these past hundred years when I wished to be human most, it was that day. Had I been there, perhaps I could have stopped him. I was a new Sleepbringer at the time, and when Chimere brought me the news, I cursed my helplessness. Though Sandmen are not permitted to leave their charges, Chimere allowed me to visit Mama's grave site during the funeral. It was on that day that I promised myself I would never, ever hesitate to act if needed, if it came to the life or death of someone I cared about.

I turn to him, the lessons of the day forgotten. "What exactly do you mean?"

CHAPTER 13
Julia

Ever since I can remember, every time I've come home, my mom has been sitting on the steps outside our front door, waiting for me. It doesn't matter that I'm sixteen, only days away from being old enough to drive and free to go where I want; I expect she'll still be this protective of me when I'm fifty, and I can't blame her. This time, she's gnawing on a celery stick. It must be, for her and my dad, "health week"; once a month, after indulging in too many Ho Hos and Twix bars, she'll go to Giant and pick up all the fixings for her own little farmers' market. We'll probably have something with tofu for dinner, but at this point, I'm glad. I ate three funnel cakes at Sweetie Pi's while contemplating the Rubik's Cube incident.

It's the same greeting she's given me every day since Griffin died: "Hon, how're you doing?" and a little shoulder rub. She swats a fly away from her face and crinkles her brow. She's the only one who can ask me how I'm feeling until her face falls off and it doesn't bother me. Maybe because I trust that she really does care about me. She really *does* want to hear the answer, good or bad.

"Good," I say as she reaches over and wipes a little gritty cinnamon sugar off my cheek, near the scars. She's the only one who can touch my scars without making me cringe. I notice an envelope sitting beside her.

She holds it out to me. "Thought this might lift your spirits."

I read the return address: *New York, New York*. It's from *Architectural Journal*'s monthlong summer program for high school students interested in pursuing engineering and architecture degrees in college—the program I was rejected from months ago, when Griffin was alive. I'd been psyched when I'd applied, at the beginning of my sophomore year, because I'd always wanted to design buildings, even when I was a kid, building skyscrapers out of Popsicle sticks in my bedroom at night. But with Griffin's help, after I'd gotten my rejection, I'd come to see *not* going as a good thing. "If you'd gone off to New York for a month, that would have blown everything," he'd said. And he was right. He was slated to go to UCLA in early August, so that wouldn't have given us any time together.

"What do they want?" I say, a little bitter, because, after all, they rejected me. Even if they begged me to come now, I wouldn't dare . . .

She shoves it into my hands. "One way to find out."

I shrug and rip the envelope open, then unfold the paper. I catch the phrases "there has been a cancellation" and "pleased to welcome you" and let out a little shriek. "They want me!" I cry.

So what if it's by default? They want me. To be in New York, the Big Apple, next month. My heart flutters at the thought.

My mom hugs me. "Oh, congrats, honey. I'm so proud of you. Your father will be so excited."

"But I can't . . . ," I say softly, and that's when I realize something. The main reason I couldn't, or wouldn't—Griffin—no longer exists. Then I look to her, seeking her approval. I know that this will be hard on her; letting me out of her sight always has been.

"Why can't you?" my mother says. "You talked nonstop about this for months."

"Really? I know. I guess I can." I suppress my smile. For some reason it seems wrong to be happy about finally getting something Griffin convinced me I didn't want. And about something that obviously must be causing my mom a minor heart attack. I mean, going to a party or working at Sweetie Pi's is one thing. Living in a whole different state for six weeks is another.

My mom says, "We'll have to go shopping to get you some city duds."

I grin. The word "shopping" has that effect on me. I picture myself on a busy city street, smiling and twirling in my new fashionable outfit, beautiful skyscrapers surrounding me. "Thanks, Mom, but are you sure?"

She nods. "You're getting your license in a few days. You're grown-up. You can take care of yourself."

This is a huge step for my mom. I hug her and head into the house. I run upstairs and throw my books and my Sweetie Pi's apron onto the bed. Then I pick up my phone and the Wilson High directory. I open it, find the number, and dial. She picks up right away, as if the phone is attached to her like her very own tumor.

"Hey, is this Ebony?" I ask.

"Yep. Who's this?"

"Julia. Hi."

There's a few seconds' pause. I know I'm probably the last person she expected to hear from. "Oh, hey, what's up?"

"Hi," I say, and then realize I'm a moron, because I said that already. So I quickly follow up with "Yeah, so that party Wednesday? Can I still go with you guys?"

I cringe; that's even more moronic. Like I'm-a-total-dweeb-and-have-no-friends-so-I-have-to-glom-on-to-you moronic. If she thinks so, though, she doesn't let on. "Sure thing, Jul," she says. Then she laughs. "You could have told me tomorrow at school. I didn't even know you had my number."

"Oh. School directory," I say lamely. She does have a point. I could have just told her in school, of course. But I was so busy riding the high of my *Architectural Journal* summer session acceptance that I momentarily lost my grasp on reality.

"Right," she says. And then there's this awkward pause. I begin to remember exactly why I had no friends before Griffin and Bret. "See you tomorrow, then," she finally adds. I can tell her finger is hovering over the "End" button on her phone.

"Oh, sure. See you." Click.

I shake off the feeling of embarrassment and lean back on my pillow. This is a *good* thing. This is what is called moving on, pushing past "Front-Page Julia," full speed ahead. I'm sure this is what Griffin would want for me.

My phone vibrates in my hand. At first I think it must be

Ebony calling back to say, "We've reconsidered. You are too much of a loser," but then I check the display. It's Bret's number. As I'm contemplating whether to answer, the ring tone begins to play.

I stare at the cell, watching my knuckles grow white around it. Because I felt like it was Griffin's last act, I never changed the ring tone from that cheesy "Ring My Bell." But this is a different song, vaguely familiar. An old song. The voice is one of those icons, Frank Sinatra or Dean Martin. I've never been crazy about that music, but . . .

Griffin was.

I put the phone down on my comforter, still unable to take my eyes from it. *"Just remember, darling, all the while . . ."*

Oh, no. Though I don't know the song, I anticipate the words before they're out.

"You belong to me."

All I want to do is stop the music. I don't want to speak to Bret, but I don't want to be alone, either. I flip open the phone. "Bret," I say, breathless.

"What were you doing, running a marathon?"

"No, I . . ." My mind is wandering so far from this place that I forget to speak at an audible volume.

"Listen," he says, oblivious. "I think I know who could have broken into my locker, if it wasn't you. Which I'm still not convinced of, by the way."

He proceeds into a long explanation about some guy on the track team who was pissed at Bret for beating his time in the last meet and whose uncle is a janitor. But all I'm thinking about is my possessed cell phone. I got a call from Bret last night, and the *"You can ring my be-e-ell"* made my skin crawl. Since then, I've had my phone in my backpack, which hasn't left my side, so . . .

"What do you think?" he asks.

"Um, I guess," I mutter. It certainly sounds better than a dead boyfriend haunting us. Though that explanation is sounding more and more reasonable by the minute.

After all, that song. That's the kind of music only Griffin liked. And he was the one constantly programming my phone with new ring tones. I think back to my dream, in which he was standing outside, in his tuxedo, fists balled. His lips were closed in a snarl, but the rage on his face spoke very clearly.

Don't forget me, he seemed to say. *You belong to me.*

CHAPTER 14
Eron

The next day, I spend my morning on the curb outside Julia's house, rather than in her tree. I can't risk turning human there and being caught "peeping" by the neighbors again; this time I am sure they would call the police, and with good reason. Out of the shade, the sun is blinding and hot. I wonder if people who don't actually exist can get sunburned.

Late in the morning, at about the same time I became human yesterday, a little girl races by on her scooter and waves at me. That's it. Showtime.

I proceed out of Julia's neighborhood. Turning to the right, I head away from the bus stop, toward the center of town. I hope that is where I will find the school.

Where I will find Julia.

I wonder how much time I will have today before I start to fade. If Chimere could see, she would not be pleased, as I'm supposed to use the minimal time I have bouncing between worlds to situate myself in my new life. Not doing this. Not clinging to charges who will no longer be my concern once I make the transition. But despite my being so far from situated in this world that I might as well be residing on the moon, I can't stop thinking about what Mr. Colburn said. *He'll hurt her.*

Today I see more of the town Julia calls home, and though the buildings are further apart, it's just as busy as the city of Newark was when I was growing up. I come to a wide, wide street, as vast as the Hudson River I remember. Across it, I see an enormous sprawling brick building. Julia's school, I presume, since she has dreamt of it once or twice. Though it is only across the street, it might as well be in another land. Standing here, I feel as small and defenseless as an insect. Motorcars are zooming by at breakneck speeds. I step from the curb several times but always scurry back to safety. A horn blares.

This is madness.

Finally, the vehicles slow to a stop. A girl in an obscene outfit that shows her middle section takes a quick look right and left and steps out into the street as if she is not taking her life in her hands. I watch to make sure she isn't killed, then scamper at her heels, her faithful shadow. Heaving a sigh, I step onto the opposite curb. Safe.

Mr. Colburn mentioned something about how Julia used to lunch on the green with him, outside. He said that they always sat at the last picnic table on the right with an enormous plate of french-fried potatoes and a Coca-Cola. It was "their" place. Now, he said, she would probably be eating alone, reading. I walk along the chain-link fence until I come to the edge of the building. On the other side of the fence, not ten feet from me, is the table he was referring to. But there are four girls sitting there.

It takes me a moment to realize that one of them *is* Julia; her hair looks more mussed than usual, though it is down in its normal style, forward over her cheeks and forehead. Her eyes are heavier, her skin paler than I usually see in the darkness, in the confines of her bedroom.

She seems anxious. Last night, we had quite the struggle getting her to sleep. My student trembled and cursed under his breath once or twice, but he kept at it, silently, steadily. There was something on her mind, but her sleep was dreamless, so it gave us no indication of what the trouble was. Colburn hadn't told me exactly *what* in the human world he'd touched, but her anxiety made me certain that it was something of Julia's, and that she'd noticed it. She is not a stupid girl, after all.

I stand there, watching for a moment, as they chat and giggle. In the sunlight, Julia glows, unlike I've ever seen. I'm used to taking in her delicate form by moonlight, so I had no idea her skin was so luminous, so pale, so fragile. She is the most reserved of all the girls, and it pleases me somewhat to see how uncomfortable she is among the group; it's just another thing we have in common. When she offers her plate of fries to the table, her voice is nearly drowned out in the breeze.

She is safe. This should be enough for me. I am but a stranger to her, and I know I shouldn't stare or else risk looking like a lunatic. But as a Sleepbringer, I had the luxury of gazing at her for as long as I wanted, and perhaps that is why I can't seem to look away.

One by one, the girls turn to me. The combination of amusement and shock on their faces is palpable. My first instinct is to run away, but before I can, Julia turns. Her eyes narrow and then widen as she takes me in. I've never before felt the weight of her eyes on mine. It's so dizzying I have to lace my fingers through the fence to steady myself. I wonder if she always has that effect on people.

I realize I am still wearing my hat—what a boor I am—and quickly remove it. "Good day," I say, and my voice quavers awfully; how disgraceful. But it has been years since I've spoken to any human female, much less four of them. I feel a trickle of sweat slide down my temple; for the first time in a hundred years, I am perspiring.

One of them, a girl with dark skin and even darker hair, straightens to get a better look at me. "Are you going to get naked?"

I turn my ear toward her, certain I'm mistaken. "Beg pardon?"

She shrugs. "Damn. I thought someone had sent us a strip-o-gram. You're *fine*."

A strip-o- . . . ? I hope they're not implying what I think they are. Julia is too young and upstanding to dabble in such things; it is a disappointment to discover that she is again choosing to surround herself with individuals who are beneath her. "Yes, I am fine, thank you very much," I answer. "How do you do?"

A moment of silence passes before they all break into laughter. I'm doing frightfully well, if my intention was to be a comic act.

I know I should just say farewell and be on my way, but something about this moment is so thrilling I can't resist. The opportunity to talk to the girl I've guided her entire life, to have her regard me as well. I remember with a stab of pain in my heart those countless decades I spent regretting never asking Gertie to the church social, the many nights I spent knowing I would do things differently, had I only the chance. I realize I'm clutching my hat to my chest so tightly I'm digging holes into the silk with my fingernails. Her name escapes my mouth naturally, since it has been on the tip of my tongue for years. "Julia."

They all look at her. Slowly, she rises from the seat, swinging her leg over the bench, and walks to me, timidly, as if being pulled against her will. She stops more than arm's distance away from the fence. It strikes me at that moment that as a human, I have always made women uneasy. I seem to threaten them just as much as they threaten me.

She's wearing a long flowered skirt; it's delicate and suits her. "Yeah?" she asks in a brusque voice that does not.

"Hello. My name is Eron DeMarchelle," I say softly, bowing my head in respect.

Behind her, one of the girls shouts in a brash tone better suited to a bartender, "Take it all off, baby!"

Julia turns to them for barely a second and then to me, blushing charmingly. "How do you know my name?"

I could tell her much more about herself, probably more than even she knows, but that is not my purpose. I smile. "You do not know me, but —"

Smack. Something, or someone, hits me on the back of the head. I recoil, wincing, and look around, rubbing the soreness on the back of my head. Nothing there. But I know better.

I clear my throat. "What I wanted to say was —"

I stop midsentence. I feel a twinge and look down at my

hands. I can see the fence and blades of grass on the ground through them, just barely. It's not quite noticeable yet, but I know what is coming. I must flee before I disappear in front of her.

"I must go," I say hurriedly.

"I . . . don't understand." Above, a bell rings, tinny and disconcerting. Julia looks away, hesitating. "I—I've got to go, too," she says, moving away from the fence. She picks up her tray and disappears into the building without another glance in my direction.

And that is when I see a face, twisted in rage, in the school's dust-coated window. The same boy from Julia's dream. Mr. Colburn's best friend.

CHAPTER 15
Julia

Breathe.

Once inside, I need to remind myself to do that. Though the air in the courtyard was fresh and cool and smelled like the honeysuckles lining the back of the school, and the air here, in the dank cafeteria, reeks of mustard, onion, and some unidentifiable dead animal, I finally have an easier time getting my lungs to work.

He spoke to me like he knew me. But I'd remember if I'd seen him before, and not just because of the top hat and spats. He's easily the best-looking guy I've ever seen, someone unforgettable. It was obvious Ebony and her crew thought the same, judging by the way they drooled into their lunch trays. He had a movie-star, chiseled jawline with the slightest hint of late-day stubble, and dark brooding eyes that lingered lazily, comfortably on me, making me uneasy. I'd have remembered very clearly a guy who could look at me that way. I had the vaguest feeling of déjà vu, but nothing I could place.

He knew my name. And he wanted to speak to me, only to me. About what? Probably that I can save hundreds on auto insurance by switching to his company. But still . . .

What kind of insurance salesman wears a tuxedo?

Before I can formulate a better explanation, an arm snakes around my shoulders and pulls me against the cold cinder block wall of the cafeteria. I gasp, then relax when I see Bret. "Who was that guy?" he asks, just a bit too loudly and too protectively for my liking.

I shrug. "No clue," I say, wondering if my cheeks are still flushed. He leans into me, so close I think he's going to put his forehead against mine. That's something Griffin used to do; he would boast that he could read my thoughts by osmosis. But Bret has never been this close, and that's when I smell his breath, hot and sour. His dad's scotch, I think. "Are you trying to get suspended on the second-to-last day of school?"

He grins, and slurs, "I'm going to B Tri-C. All you need to get in there are three brain cells and a number two pencil."

This is nothing new to me. Bret is constantly disparaging himself because Griffin got into a good school and he didn't. Bret has never been the scholarly type, so that's why he's going to Bucks County Community College this fall. And when he's drunk, he likes to mope and feel sorry for himself. "Oh, stop," I say, slapping him lightly. "Look on the bright side."

He's still standing entirely too close for my liking. And looking entirely too serious. The smile is still there, but barely. Unfortunately, Bret gets that way when he drinks. He raises an eyebrow. "And what is the bright side, Ippie?"

"You know. You won't be here, at Wilson."

His face falls until only a trace of a smile is left. Clearly it was not the answer he was hoping for. He sighs and his eyes trail to the ground. "I always thought the bright side was that I would be near you."

I'm trying to figure out how I can escape him, so it takes me a moment to realize what he has said. I search for the irony, the sarcasm in his features, but there is none. He's not looking at me; though he may be tipsy, he's obviously still aware that he's out of his comfort zone. Bret is being *sweet*. How can I run away and toss a casual "See you" over my shoulder when he's baring his soul like this? I can't. But I can't think of anything else to say, so a lame "Oh" slips out.

Maybe a full minute passes, and I still can't think of anything to say. Well, nothing nice. I can think of a hundred insults, the best being "Go tell it to Dr. Phil," thanks to all the time I spent with Griffin.

Finally, he mumbles, "I thought with Griffin gone, you and I would be . . . you and I . . . we make sense. But you're . . . changing. . . . I mean, don't you like me anymore?"

It's really pathetic. He sounds like a three-year-old asking if someone, anyone, will play with him on the playground. But this is Bret; he's only this way because he's drinking. Tomorrow he'll shrug it off and crack jokes about it. "It's not you," I explain, knowing I'm heading for that horrible cliché *It's not you, it's me*. "You know I loved Griffin. I still do. And—"

My mouth is still forming words when he swoops in and lays a kiss on it. His lips are cold and wet and lacking all muscle tone, like two fat jellyfish. And I thought it wasn't possible for a kiss to be any less passionate than in my dream. But how can I deny a guy who has just broken open a vein for me like that? He brings his hand to my cheek and strokes it, kind of nice and soft, like I'm some fine treasured possession, so I know this is a big deal for him. Even if he will deny that tomorrow. So I tilt my chin up and kiss back. But only for a second, because at that moment someone tweaks my ass.

"Ouch!" we both shout in unison, separating.

I rub my backside, muttering curses, ready to slap him, when I realize that one of Bret's hands is wrapped around a jug of something probably laced with scotch, and the other, the one that was previously stroking my cheek, is now gingerly massaging the back of his head. "Something hit me," he moans, sour-faced. He turns around, looking confused. The vast cafeteria is empty except for a couple of hairnetted ladies cleaning tables in the far corner.

I stop rubbing as a tingling sensation rises up my neck to my hairline. Only one person I know liked to squeeze my butt like that.

Oh, hell.

I belong to you. I belong to you, Griffin, I say to myself, as if he's in my mind and can hear my thoughts. I start to move away from Bret, but he grabs my hand. "Are you okay?"

I snatch it back. Any more physical contact and my backside might end up a black-and-blue checkerboard. "Yeah. Late for class," I say, forcing a smile.

It's crazy. Crazy to think Griffin is still here.

Still, when I turn away from Bret and make my way past the empty tables, I mutter, almost inaudibly, "I belong to you, Griffin."

Just in case.

CHAPTER 16
Eron

Twenty, twenty-five minutes. At the most.

By the time I'm back on Julia's front lawn, I'm in a dither. It's less than five days before I'm supposed to return to the human world for good. By now, my time on earth should be stretching to at least three or four hours each day. Instead, I barely had time to orient myself before fading. And all because of my student, who can't for the life of him follow simple directions.

I grimace, rubbing my sore head. If he hadn't swatted me there, I might have had a few more moments with Julia. His interference with the human world caused me to fade. I am certain of it. If he is not behaving himself like a proper Sleepbringer, then I cannot be human.

Before I can climb Julia's tree, I hear Chimere's giggles. Here I thought she'd be in a sour mood like me, scolding our newest member for his transgressions. Sometimes I just don't understand her. When I rise past the leaves to the branch she's lounging on, I realize that she's not just in a joyful mood; she's in a joyful mood because my student is . . . Oh, how improper.

Chimere has her shoe off, and her skirt is pulled up to her knee. And Mr. Colburn is sitting across from her, leaning against the trunk of the tree, with her foot in his lap. Massaging her ankle. They turn to me, and immediately Chimere blushes and throws her skirt down to cover more of her legs. She giggles some more. "I twisted my ankle," she explains, "and Mr. Colburn was good enough to tend to it."

"The saint," I mutter.

She tilts her head. "Oh! What has gotten you in such a foul mood?"

I jab a finger at the young man at the other end of her branch. He's much too absorbed in Chimere's tender and dainty foot for my liking. It's shameful. "He has," I say, seething. "I should still be down there, becoming human. Instead, I had no more than thirty minutes."

Colburn's eyes narrow. "Just what are you accusing me of, old man?"

A vein on the side of my brow pulsates with heat. Chimere straightens. "Don't fret, my pet. Everything is in order."

"In order? How can you—"

"Mr. Colburn did well with the seduction last night, did he not? I was very pleased. And do not trouble yourself if you were only human a short time today. These things vary. Everything will come together," she says soothingly.

It's infuriating. I seem to recall Chimere being much less indulgent when I was learning the trade. They stare at me until my cheeks burn. "But . . . he hit me," I sputter, very aware that I sound every bit of two years old.

"What the hell are you talking about?" he returns indignantly. Oh, what I wouldn't give to slap that smug expression off his lying face.

"Nonsense, Eron," Chimere sings, turning to him. "He has been here, with me. For quite some time."

They exchange looks, and I can tell someone is not being truthful. Perhaps they are both lying. I've always trusted Chimere, though she can be naive, but she is not above telling lies. She hates conflict. Her eyes turn to me, pleading.

I sigh. "Fine, fine," I say to Chimere. "But tell him. Make sure he knows that he can't touch humans. If he gets sent to the Last Place and I'm stuck here, I'll—"

Colburn exhales. "I get it, I get it. See that dead horse in the corner?"

Chimere smiles. "It looks like we are all in accordance. I'll leave you both to your work, then. Please try to get along."

I meet Colburn's sneer with an icy glare. We don't speak for several moments. Finally, he says, "Sure we will."

Even after Chimere disappears, we continue our staring match. I sigh. "Why did you hit me?"

"I was trying to show you. Bret was in the window, watching you, and—"

"I know."

"So then you know what I said was true." I'm about to say that I'm still unsure, when his face softens. "So was it me hitting you that shortened your time down there?"

"I imagine so."

He shakes his head. "Bret had his hands all over her today."

"He . . . did?" The thought alarms me, but I push it away. This is not something we need be concerned about. "Well, perhaps that is what she wants."

"No way in hell. You didn't see the look on her face. She was just being nice."

He does have a point. Julia is nothing if not polite, but she *did* cry out against him when he kissed her in her dream. "Still . . . I have a hard time believing that this young man, your best friend, can be as evil as you say."

His eyes narrow. "Why would I lie?"

"Because you are obviously too attached to her to be thinking straight."

"Oh yeah?" He rubs his chin, and his face falls, revealing him in a rare vulnerable moment. Clearly hurt, he mutters, "Screw you."

Everything he says blurs the line between truth and fiction. If Julia truly is in danger . . . if I knew that for certain, I couldn't stand idly by. I didn't before; though I knew it was against the rules, my emotions got the best of me. Colburn's face reveals nothing, but I don't need to take his word for it, I suppose. I have the answers at my disposal. It will take some careful research, perhaps require the bending of a few rules, but the answers are there.

I give him a pointed look. "Fine. I will check into it. If you follow the rules."

He nods. "Fine."

"I'm quite serious. If I so much as suspect you're not where you should be, I won't do a thing."

He sighs. "Got it. I promise."

Since he's almost sounding reasonable, I go further. "And please don't play with Chimere like that. She may be an Original but she's quite naive to humans."

He grins. "Are you jealous, old man?"

I straighten, thinking of how she let him do something so compromising as massaging her foot. "Of course not. It's simply . . . I can tell she has taken a liking to you, and I would hate to see her hurt."

"Seriously?" He grins. "But you said she's not interested in that. She's not a girl."

"You are not a man," I remind him. I'm relieved when the door to Julia's room opens and I see her enter, then settle down on the bed. Though it's a warm June day, she pulls the comforter over her body. The sun is setting, but still strong, streaming orange rays through her blinds. It's much too early for Julia to be sleeping. And yet I can feel that it's time. The compulsion to visit her is overwhelming, drawing me toward her window. My student inches forward, feeling the drive as well. He casts me a questioning look, and I shrug. "I suppose," I say, following him through the window and into the bedroom.

We separate and move over her, one of us on each side of her bed. Only her forehead and a few wisps of her tea-colored hair are poking out from the blankets. I gently ease the sheets down and study her. There are deep worry lines in her brow, and her jaw seems clenched in pain. "Is she ill?" I ask, mostly to myself. I bring my hand over her forehead but feel no heat there.

But there's no mistake, I realize, as I look at her hands clutching her pink comforter, that she's trembling.

I meet my student's eyes. He gives me the same wide-eyed expression he wore when I accused him of lying to Chimere.

I draw in a breath. "Mr. Colburn. What did you do to her?"

In the early morning, satisfied that Mr. Colburn is doing what needs to be done to care for our charges, I make my way across town, checking every so often to see if Chimere has followed me. Again, she will not be pleased to know what I am up to, but this is something I am compelled to do as Julia's protector.

I stop at a large brick house I know only vaguely. Once or twice, when Julia didn't come home, I was drawn here, only to find her yawning away on the leather sofa in the basement. Perhaps Mr. Colburn and Mr. Anderson had been nearby, but I'd never seen them. This time, I venture to the window of Bret's bedroom. A girl with white-blond hair is perched on the landing, and she's dressed so revealingly I can't bring myself to look at her. Her breasts spill out of her tight red dress, which barely covers any part of her long legs. She narrows her eyes at me as I approach.

"Good morning," I say.

She doesn't answer; she's too busy inspecting me, clearly wondering why I've come. As I've said, this is solitary work.

I know she isn't going to like what I have to say, so I speak in my friendliest voice. "You may leave. I'm going to take care of your charge until he wakes."

She moves in front of the window. "Hell you will. Bret Anderson is mine."

I can tell she's new to the seduction. I haven't had much interaction with the new ones, other than Mr. Colburn, but besides their less than adequate formal dress, they can be so crass. So boorish. And so overly possessive. "There is a . . . rather perplexing situation. I don't have time to explain, but I should like to read his dreams. He will be perfectly safe."

She stiffens. "That's not allowed!" she spews, but I can tell she's thinking, Or is it?

I move closer to the window, and she scurries away like a frightened mouse, still grimacing at me. I pass inside, into a dark room. Mr. Anderson has not yet woken. He's snoring loudly and the room smells like old cigarettes and alcohol. I move to the side of the bed and put my hand over his head.

The dream is horrific. In it, he's with Julia, and so much of her pale skin is visible I can only gasp. Her makeup is heavy and her features are distorted in such a way that she looks cheap and obscene, almost like Evangeline. Her body is pressed against Mr. Anderson's and I can barely tell where she ends and he begins. He's running his tongue along her neck and she's making a horrible, animal noise I've never imagined someone like Julia could make. But this is *his* dream. This is how he sees her, as wrong as it is. I pull myself out quickly, my body hot with rage. When I turn to the window and pass the blond girl outside, she is studying her fingernails. The shadows darken her face, but she is grinning, triumphant, happy to see me speechless as I slip away.

• • •

Mr. Colburn joins me as I'm trembling on the sidewalk outside Julia's house, thinking about Bret Anderson's dream. As much as I hate to admit it, he was right. When I tell him this, his face twists. "How do I protect her, then?"

"You warn her, in her dreams. That is the best you can do."

"That's not enough. I tried to get through to her last night, and she didn't listen."

"She was in quite an agitated state. Something you created, mind you. And if she isn't willing to listen, there's nothing you can do."

"There is *something* I can do," he whispers, his eyes sparkling like firecrackers. "Something you can do, actually. You are going to be human."

I don't like the wild look in his eyes. He had it when he tried to seduce Julia, and I am not at all comfortable with it. "And?"

"I may not be able to protect her. But you can."

I remember the way she looked at me when I introduced myself. It was so cold. "I'm but a stranger to her. She'd never believe me."

His eyes are intent. "Tell her it's a message from me."

This is what I was afraid of. "That is completely out of the question. Chimere would be—"

"Saint DeMarchelle. Afraid of getting your hand slapped by the old lady, are you?"

I glare at him.

"Why did you go to the school, anyway, old man?" he says, prodding. "You weren't just passing through. You wanted to see if what I said was the truth. You went there to protect her."

"No, I . . . ," I begin, but I know that the truth is written everywhere on me. It's in my nature to protect her. It's something I cannot *not* do.

He moves so that his face is level with mine, and presses his palms together. "You want her to be safe, don't you?"

I don't answer. He knows already. He knows what buttons of mine to press. And though I promised myself, promised Chimere, I'd never disobey the rules again, I can already feel my resolve weakening. That is not a promise I can keep.

Something dawns on me as a slow smile spreads on his face. He can see my strength crumbling. "It would be a shame if I wasn't able to take your place, wouldn't it? I mean, if I can't manage my duties as a Sandman? If I get thrown in the Last Place? You would be stuck up here for another hundred years, right?"

I nod, the heat rising in my neck. "But you wouldn't . . ."

He laughs and looks up at the pink clouds swirling through the early-dawn sky. "If you don't help me, you bet your ass I would."

CHAPTER 17
Julia

A car horn beeps in my driveway, right on time, but by then, I've been sitting in the hallway for a full twenty minutes, twiddling my thumbs anxiously. I almost called to cancel with Ebony about fifty times, but then I decided I was just being stupid. Everything that had happened to remind me of Griffin was only a coincidence. That is the most logical explanation, and a hell of a lot more believable than the idea that his ghost is haunting me. School is out. I should be happy. Instead, for the past two days, I've been walking around scared of my own shadow, when in two weeks I'll be going to New York City. Growing up. This is no time to slink back into being the poor victim that everyone thinks I am.

I slide into the backseat, next to two other girls. Ebony is driving, and the girl in the front passenger seat, Gloria, is smoking a cigarette. When Ebony speeds away, the hair I spent an hour trying to get just right blows around like a tumbleweed, in a cloud of thick smoke. Perfect. As I'm smoothing it down, Ebony glances at me in the rearview mirror. "So we've all been talking about you. And we want to know. Give us the scoop."

My first thought is Oh, God, they saw the kiss. The kiss that I've regretted since the second it happened. I didn't even need a pinch in the ass for that. Luckily, since then, Bret has probably been too busy recovering from his hangover and preparing to walk the football field in his cap and gown to track me down. "Um, what?"

"Duh. The hot guy at lunch?"

Oh, him. I'd almost been able to forget him. Well, sort of. I still catch my breath when I remember those gorgeous dark eyes. But there is really nothing to tell. I convinced myself that he had the wrong Julia. "I have no idea who he is," I say.

The girls sigh collectively. Clearly they were looking for some good dirt. The one next to me, Amber, laughs, and I can smell something fruity on her breath. Peach schnapps. I think they already started drinking, without me. She says, "I was hoping he was your long-lost brother or something, and you could fix me up."

Ebony turns onto Main Street. "He was *fine*. I still think he was a stripper. He looked like he had a nice bod under that tux. What did he say to you?"

"Nothing really."

"Oh, wow. Totally mysterious. Maybe it *was* a strip-o-gram. Too bad the bell rang before he got naked for us."

I shrug, doubtful. The guy was hot, but stiff; he didn't look like he was ready to peel off his tuxedo shirt. Besides, who on earth would send me a strip-o-gram? Griffin, maybe. No, not possible. It was a mistake. That's all. He just had the wrong girl.

When we arrive at the party, I look up at the stately white colonial. All windows are lit, and I can see the outlines of people. It's almost like the walls are pulsing in beat with the music coming from inside. Screams and shouts emanate from the brightly lit backyard. I hold my hands together, since they are about to drip sweat onto my denim skirt. Every party I've ever been to, I was cut off from the rest of the world. I had my two bookends, my two buffers, shielding me from the outside. Now I can't stop quivering. It's nerves, yes, but something more. Excitement. Before, my outlook was limited, but now anything can happen.

Amber wraps her arms around Gloria and the other girl and they stumble toward the front of the house. Yep, definitely drunk. I follow them like a tail, wishing I had the guts to join in. Ebony stuffs her keys into her wristlet and says, "Let's get this party started."

The second we get inside, my body is smashed up against the wall. It's that crowded. I try to follow Ebony, but she's so tiny that she squeezes between two football-player frames and disappears into the mass of bodies. Great. I'm not sure what gave me the impression when Ebony said we should go together that we'd actually *stay* together. All the people in the room, pressed together like they are, look foreign, like students from some other school. They still seem to be enjoying themselves; I can barely breathe. I begin to wonder if it's possible for me to survive a party without Griffin and Bret. I push my way through, into the kitchen. It's not much better here, but there's an open door across the way, and I can feel the night breeze on my forehead. I push forward, being knocked here and there, until finally, I put my hand on the knob of the screen door and throw it open. Freedom.

Quickly, I step down, toward the massive in-ground pool, wishing I had someone, anyone, to save me, even . . .

"Hey, you."

Even Bret.

"Hi," I say, relieved, thinking, So what? Being with Bret is definitely better than being completely alone. "Congratulations, Mr. High School Graduate." I throw a hand onto his chest, not meaning to suggest anything, but he takes it and starts to massage it. He doesn't speak. He's just smiling dumbly, swaying to the music, eyes half closed. And that's when I realize something. He's not swaying to the music. He's swaying as in ready to topple over. And his eyes are half closed, as in two steps away from dreamland. He's falling-down drunk.

"Bret," I say. "Let's go sit down."

"Oh, yeah yeah yeah," he slurs, pulling me by the wrist. We pass plenty of open lawn chairs, but he keeps tugging me, nearly falling over the side of a miniature wooden bridge into the koi pond below, before leading me into a darkened cabana room. There are two couches, and when I realize they're both occupied by couples doing things I probably shouldn't be an audience to, I look away from them, embarrassed. He escorts me toward a mat that's been set up on the ground, all cozy and covered with pillows. As if he was expecting to take me here. Reluctantly, I follow, then manage to set him down and stand over him. I don't know what he's thinking, probably a whole lot of nothing.

"You should just rest here," I say. I make a move to leave, but then I realize I don't have anywhere to go.

He reaches up from the pillows and yanks on my hand. "Stay."

I sigh. "Fine," I say, and kneel down next to him, trying not to get too close or too comfortable. But he has other plans. He moves in. I shift my body away from his.

"Julia." He says my name so singsongy, so passionately, I have to laugh. It's not possible to be that drunk and still be romantic. But he keeps trying. He strokes my face. "You are so gorgeous."

I squirm away. "Stop, Bret. Just rest."

"I don't want to," he says, his tone changing. Suddenly, he sounds annoyed. "Stop saying that."

"You're drunk."

"I'm not so drunk that I don't know what I want." When I see his face in a sliver of light filtering through a cabana window, he looks really pissed, worse than I've ever seen him. Then he leans toward me again, going in for a kiss.

"We can't," I say, giving his chest a little shove back.

"Why not? Don't you get it? Griffin and you . . . never would have worked. He was going away. I'll be here. We can—"

"I'm going away," I tell him. "I'm going to the city in two weeks, for the rest of the summer. For the *Architectural Journal.*"

His eyes narrow. "What? I thought you—"

"I know, but I got in. There was a cancellation."

This is where any ordinary friend would be happy for me. Instead, Bret's face sinks in misery. That smile—the permanently glued one—has peeled from his face. He looks around haggardly, like he's trying to find something to throw, and then his eyes focus on me. "You can't. You *can't,*" he moans, his voice climbing an octave.

"I'm going to, Bret."

"Fine! And I'll be stuck here, in Loserville. Alone."

He looks at his feet, and I sit there awkwardly. As a good friend, I should be offering him compassion. So I reach over and wrap my arm around him. And that's when he turns and clamps his wet mouth on mine. This time, it feels exactly like it did in the dream, like a vacuum, sucking me dry. He grabs me by the shoulders and then pushes me back, pinning me against the mat. I'm so shocked that I'm caught breathless as he grinds his body against mine. I try to say something, to scream, but his mouth is on mine and he's stealing all those words from me. The most I can manage is a muffled "Stop," but it's so powerless that it doesn't have any effect.

At once, the pressure is lifted. I open my eyes, but my sight is blurred. "I believe she asked you to stop," a voice, edged with authority, says.

An angel? Griffin?

My vision clears, but in the darkness, all I can make out is the outline of Bret, breathing hard. Someone is holding him by the arms. He struggles to release himself, then shakes himself loose from the hold he's in, spilling his beer. It's wet between my toes. The other figure pushes him toward the door of the cabana, away from me. I see Bret's face, white like the moon, in the minimal light, but it's blank of all understanding of what has just happened. Finally, he mutters, "Jules . . . ," but he can't seem to get anything else out. He staggers away, head down, leaving me alone with this stranger.

His frame is smaller than Griffin's, though he's just as tall. He moves closer, extends a hand to me. The light streaming through the window casts an aura upon his back, yes, just like an angel.

In the dark, all I can make out is that he's wearing a suit jacket. He's very well dressed—too well dressed for a high school graduation party.

I take his hand, and as he pulls me to my feet, he murmurs to me, "Julia, I have a message for you."

CHAPTER 18
Eron

I lead Julia out of the cabana. I realize it's the first time in sixteen years that I've ever touched her skin. It feels just as I imagined: warm, smooth. Her fingers are delicate and thin, like flower stems.

She's still trembling, babbling, trying to smooth down her hair. When we're in the moonlight, she drops my hand, seeming self-conscious. "Bret's a good friend of mine," she explains. "He's just drunk. I am sure he didn't realize what he was doing."

I shake my head. My fists are still clenched. As Mr. Anderson slinks away, I see my stepfather's cruel face on his body. Mr. Colburn was right. "You do not know what he was thinking."

She squints at me. "And you do?"

"I—" I begin. "No, I just—" I hold my tongue when I realize I appear more mentally unstable than Bret Anderson.

"But thank you," she says. "You're that guy from school yesterday. You have a message for me?"

"Yes," I say. I'm fairly certain Mr. Colburn is with his

charges, holding up his end of the promise. There is no chance he would have let his best friend take such liberties with his girlfriend without interfering himself had he been watching. So now is the time for me to hold to my promise. "You . . . you need to be careful. To stay away from people like that."

"Like I said, he's my friend." She wraps her arms around herself and lets out a short laugh. "Was that a message from my mom?"

"No, actually . . ." I stop before I can get out the words. My mouth knows what to say—*It's a message from Griffin Colburn*—but my head won't let me say it. She's still trembling. I think back to last night, when we were luring her to sleep and she quivered in the same way. Clearly she is in no state to hear this news. Not now. "It's not exactly a message. It's more of an observation. Er . . . you need to be careful." I feel my face growing hot; this is all too familiar ground that I'm treading on. I sound like a fool, like I always have with women.

"Bret wouldn't have hurt me," she repeats.

"He would have," I mutter, thinking of Mama. She said the same thing about my stepfather. *He may not always act good, but he's a good man.*

"How do you know? Who are you, anyway? Why is it any business of yours?"

I forget that though I've known her since she was an infant, I'm still a stranger to her. This is frightfully awkward. "It's obvious you need some looking after, if you consider that young man to be a friend."

She sighs and scans the yard. "It was a mistake coming here. I've got to go."

"Allow me to escort you home," I offer.

She gives me a sour look. "You could be a serial killer for all I know. I can take care of myself."

"Oh?" I say, pointing a thumb toward the cabana.

"At least I know Bret." She studies me. Curse that Harmon for not having suitable attire for me; it puts me at quite the disadvantage. "Are you from the museum or something?"

"No. I'm not from around here."

"Obviously." We both turn toward a commotion as someone dives into the pool across the yard, splashing several young ladies, who shriek and scream. Julia turns back to me, her face forlorn, and takes a step backward, toward the gate. "Really, thanks. But no thanks. I'm tired. I'd better be going home."

I'm not human enough yet to have lost my sense of her needs. She's so riled up by adrenaline that she's nowhere near sleep. Still, I don't think she would be happy if I told her that. "Sleep is very important," I agree.

She lets out another short laugh. "Are you sure you're not conspiring with my mom?"

"I do not understand what you are suggesting."

She mutters, "Sometimes I think she's not from this planet, either," and turns away from me. She unlocks the latch on the gate, pushes it open, and slips beyond.

It's impossible simply to turn away, to forget someone whose life I have valued more than my own for sixteen years. Since I am the one who didn't believe Mr. Colburn when he said she was in danger, the least I can do is make sure his beloved is returned safely to her bedroom. So I follow at a distance as she hurries down the street, her hands in the pockets of her jacket.

Several blocks pass. I tread softly in the grass, and she never turns to look back at me, so at first I think that she doesn't know I'm there. Then, in a streetlight, she stops. She doesn't turn around, just shouts out at the night sky, "Could you please leave me alone?"

"I'm sorry. I didn't mean to bother you," I say, walking toward her.

She whirls around, her face blank.

"I want to make sure you return safely home," I explain. "Where I am from, a gentleman never lets a lady walk alone at night."

She raises an eyebrow. "Gentleman?"

I catch my breath. Is that an obscure word these days? "Ye-es."

"Well, I'm almost home," she says. I know it's a lie, as I could find her house in a blizzard. Sandmen have a strong tie to the homes of their charges; I feel comfort and security, as from a familiar blanket, whenever I'm near one. I don't feel it at all now, and I doubt it is because I'm becoming more human, because I felt it strongly only last night.

I can't very well tell her that, so I say, "I see," and let her continue. I follow, as before.

A few blocks later, she whirls around again. I see a small light in her hand; it's her portable telephone. "I have my cell. Nine-one-one is being dialed as we speak."

"Nine-one-one?" I wonder aloud. Is that a new way of referring to the telephone?

She sticks out her chin. "I am calling the police," she answers, her face saying, *Perhaps you've heard of them?*

I hold up my hands. "Oh, no. Please. No need. I'm simply returning to my home as well."

"Where do you live?"

"Hart Avenue," I say. It's not necessarily the truth but it's not a lie, either. And though I've been there only once, I am nearly sure that Hart is in this direction.

"Oh." She continues on, silent, this time faster. She's quite athletic and jogging at a steady pace, so I find it difficult to keep up. My muscles ache; they haven't been tested in such a way in a hundred years. Ten minutes pass. I huff like a locomotive, wondering if I will survive the next few blocks to her home. Then, just when I'm certain she'll run into her house and shut the door without another word to me, oblivious to my panting and dying on her front lawn, she calls back, "What's with the strange clothes?"

I smile through my labored breath, pleased to be making progress. "Where I'm from, *you'd* be the one dressed strangely."

Thank goodness, she slows a bit. "And what planet is that, again?"

"Er. Canada."

"Canada?" she asks, her brow wrinkling. "Are you here visiting someone?"

"No, I have . . . relocated here," I say. "If you can suggest a place of employment, I'm looking for work."

"What kind of work can you do?"

"My previous job was at a textile mill. I was a picker."

"A picker? What's that?" she calls back. Then, without

waiting for a response, she says, "You can work in the mall. They're always hiring."

"The . . . mall?"

She stops, turns toward me. "Don't they have malls in Canada?"

I hope she can't see how breathless and weak I am from this distance. I shake my head.

She shrugs. "Interesting." Then she turns back again, and I resume my chase. Finally, at the walk beside her house, she points, as if I don't have every last shingle and blade of grass outside it memorized. "This is me."

I nod, and just in time, because when she turns back to me, I feel a twinge. Looking down, I can barely see my hands. My body was twitching and aching so much from the exertion that I didn't realize I was already beginning to fade. Luckily, it's too dark for her to notice anything, or else I'm sure her screams would have woken half the neighborhood by now. "Good night, Julia," I say quickly. "Sleep well."

She gives me a quick nod and hurries inside. A few minutes later, light floods her bedroom window. I wait a few moments, until I've completely faded, then scale the tree. Mr. Colburn is there, at his post, chewing on his lip, watching her. He sees me coming up and offers a hand to hoist me to a nearby branch. "And?" he asks.

I nod. "You were right. About that friend of yours."

"What?" His voice is ragged. "Did he hurt her?"

"No. But he might have, had I gotten there a moment later." He's standing up, getting ready to climb down the tree. "Where are you going?"

"To his house. I'm going to put him to sleep. Forever."

I grab him by the sleeve of his tuxedo jacket. "You'll do no such thing. You will surely go to the Last Place."

"But see? I told you he was no good for her. So you let her know? About me?"

"No," I say. He whips his head around and focuses on me, jaw tightening. I can tell he doesn't know how to deal with disappointment; he's used to getting his way. "I delivered the message. But she has already been through quite an ordeal. I didn't see how telling her of you would improve things."

"You don't get it. It *will*," he says. "She needs to know I'm there for her."

Despite his being correct about Mr. Anderson, it's still obvious that this is more about helping himself and less about helping Julia. She doesn't need to know of his existence as much as he *wants* her to. "You actually believe that her knowing you're there will make her feel safer?"

"Yeah. You don't?"

"Well, certainly," I say, my voice dripping with sarcasm. "She'll probably check herself into an insane asylum because she's hearing the voice of her dead boyfriend. I suppose she'll be *very* safe there."

He threads a small twig from the tree through his fist, pulling off all the leaves. "You don't know her like I do."

That is true, I think. I know her much better. "Mr. Colburn, things between you and Julia will never be the same again, even if you could let her know you're watching her. I am sure you are not so selfish as to put your own vanity ahead of the happiness of others."

He's silent.

"Let her live her life."

For a moment I think that perhaps my words are penetrating that thick skull of his. Then he says, "Bret has it coming to him."

I see the gears in his head turning, and I don't like it one bit. "Mr. Colburn, if you hope to become one of us, there is nothing you can do."

"You said Sandmen protect their charges. But you're going to let him get away with what he did? You know he'll do it again. Julia's too nice. Too naive."

"It's not that," I say, but even as the words come out, I know he is right. Even as I argued with her, she was protecting Mr. Anderson, calling him her friend. She has no idea what she's up against. "If you put him to sleep forever, you will ruin my chance at becoming human, and your chance of assuming your powers," I say softly.

"But," he says, "if *you* were the one who put him to sleep . . ."

I meet his eyes in the darkness. "What makes you think I'd risk—"

"Because you've done it before," he says, grinning triumphantly.

I swallow. "What . . . what do you . . ."

"Chimere covered for you, right?" He shrugs. "Too bad she isn't the best at keeping secrets."

I clench my fists. Cursed Chimere!

"I didn't know you had it in you, old man. You could have gone to the Last Place for years, if Chimere had told the elders. But she didn't. You're her pet, right? Still . . . I think the elders would be very interested if I told them, don't you? You'd both end up in the Last Place. Right?"

I think about the last human whose life I ended, all those years ago. I suffered, yes, but even now I'd do it again, and again, if I had the choice. And looking at Mr. Colburn, his face red with rage, I know that he isn't bluffing. I know that if he had the opportunity, he would damn both me and Chimere to the Last Place to protect Julia. I know he'd go there himself if he had to.

Perhaps we have more in common than I thought.

I whisper, "Yes. I will take care of it."

Julia was seven when she was kidnapped by a horrible monster and made to spend three days in a dark, dirty trailer. I'm not sure how or why this creature selected her; all I know is that one morning, she and her mother left the house on a shopping trip, and that afternoon, her mother returned, alone and frantic. And when I sought out Julia to perform my duties, I found her whimpering in fear, curled into a ball on the floor of the vehicle, not three miles from her home. The man didn't hurt her, other than scraping one gash in her cheek for every day he kept her. I saw his dreams. I know that he planned to do much worse to her, to hurt her in unspeakable ways. Ways I didn't think possible.

I spent two days watching over her, keeping her safe. Keeping her asleep so she wouldn't be afraid. So that every remaining night she spent on this earth wouldn't be filled with nightmares.

But I knew how it would end if I did nothing.

After Mama, I simply could not stand by and let those despicable things happen to Julia. Not when I had the power to stop them.

I knew I had to take care of him.

And so I know, all too well, what Mr. Colburn must be feeling. Mr. Anderson sleeps as I stare over him, readying myself to perform the seduction. Readying myself to end his life. My hands shake. I spent my entire trip here hoping that the second time, it would be easier. But, no. I turn away, feeling my heart hammering in my chest. No.

The monster in the trailer dreamt of hurting Julia. I saw the knives. I could see his memories of other girls he'd hurt, and I could sense that he was proud of that. I look around Mr. Anderson's room, hoping to find something, anything, to convince me that this boy is a monster as well. But there is nothing . . . just running trophies, pictures of performers, piles of classic novels and books on rocketry and science . . . It all seems so typical and benign. That is when I notice something on the bulletin board behind his desk. Pictures of Julia, all of them smiling down at me. There are some pictures of Mr. Colburn as well, but for the most part, they are Julia. In one, it's just Julia and Mr. Anderson . . . and someone has drawn a heart around it.

I turn to him. *Julia was right. You* wouldn't *have hurt her. You're in love with her.*

My body quivers. What was I thinking? Mr. Colburn clearly has no idea what he is asking. Ending a life is not something to take lightly. This is a boy, not even a man. He can redeem himself. I had no hope of using my powers as Sleepbringer to save Julia from that madman in the trailer;

she was trapped. Luring that man to death was my only choice.

But Bret Anderson is not the same threat to Julia. And if he does try to hurt her . . . in a few days, I will be human. I can devote my life to ensuring her safety.

That will be my unfinished business.

I take the sand from my pocket and spread more than the normal share over him. As it settles, I whisper in his ear, "If you ever see Julia again, you will apologize profusely. And you will never, *ever* lay another finger on her. Understood?"

He tosses his head and mumbles a yes.

The girl with the white-blond hair fumes at me. "What was that all about?" She runs to him, puts her hand over his forehead. "He's going to sleep all day now."

I nod and step to the window. "Exactly."

CHAPTER 19
Julia

"**M**om," I say, "I would feel a little more confident about my abilities if you would remove your foot from the dashboard."

My mother has been pressing her sandal-clad foot so hard against the glove compartment that I think she might leave an indentation. She pushes down so hard that her baby pink–polished toes turn white every time she wants me to brake. "Sorry, hon."

She removes her foot, but slowly, and only for a second. When I stop at the next light, it pops above the seat again, toes peeking up like pretty pink soldiers readying for attack. "Mom!"

She shrugs. "You're a lead foot. Just like your dad."

"No, I'm not. I'm just late for work," I explain, counting the hours until I'll be able to drive alone, until I won't have to con my mom into taking me for "practice" drives. Three days. Just slightly over seventy-two hours.

I drive down Main. It's the quickest shot to the mall, though I've avoided it. I'm sure the tree is still there, with a massive bite in its side, just like I saw in the newspaper, but without Griffin's mangled Mustang. I guess the wreckage is gone, but they wouldn't uproot a tree. It wasn't the tree's fault, after all.

I try to keep my eyes straight ahead when we pass it, but of course we stop at a light, and there it is, staring at me. The white wound in the black bark is a hideous smile, taunting me. I imagine blood, pieces of Griffin's bone burrowed permanently in that tree. I wonder if it was the last thing he ever saw. I take a breath. A car horn blares.

"Light's green," my mom reminds me gently. From her tone, I can tell she knows what I'm thinking about.

"Oh." I press on the accelerator too quickly. The car bucks a little. Whoops. "Sorry."

She kneads my shoulder, pats my knee. I feel goose bumps there prickling against her smooth hand.

We pull up to the mall entrance, and I throw the car into park, open the door, and start to slide out. Health week is clearly over, because my mother decides to climb over the console to the driver's seat. If she were still in fitness mode, she would have gotten out and jogged around the car. She struggles a little, groaning and letting out a big "oof" as she plops into the driver's seat. "Pick you up at nine. We can practice your night driving," she says, not sounding very thrilled by the prospect. Seeing the place where Griffin met his end probably has that effect on lots of parents.

I hurry through the entrance to the food court, shuddering so much at the thought of that horrible smile in the tree that I plow right into a gigantic potted plant next to Sweetie Pi's. I've gone this route across the mall a hundred times, and the plant is so big it probably can be seen from outer space, and yet I manage to jam my shin into it. When I pull my leg away and crouch over it, wishing I'd worn pants instead of shorts, I see another hideous smile there, this one red. It's already oozing blood, and on my pale gooseflesh it looks like the mouth of a vampire. Pretty.

Before I can wonder if anyone saw my latest act of stupidity, somebody is standing over me with a messy pile of little paper napkins. I take them and press them against my shin, then look up. It's Mr. I-Have-a-Message-for-You-That's-Not-Really-a-Message. From the party. "Hello," he says, handing me more napkins.

"Oh. Hi," I say. Great, he's stalking me. Maybe I shouldn't have been such a moron and told him to find work at the mall. *My* mall.

I blot the wound a little more and stand up. He has lost the tuxedo—well, kind of. He's still wearing the white shirt, with sleeves rolled up, and the dark pants with spats. The shirt is un-buttoned at the neck, which suits him. Oh, hell, he'd look hot in a chicken suit. But then I notice he's wearing a white apron with blue printing on the front, just like mine. A Sweetie Pi's apron.

I swallow, trying to remember if I ever told him where I work. No, I'm pretty sure I didn't. There are four hundred stores in this mall, and yet he manages to get a job at my place of employ-ment? This is all too creepy. But my heart begins to flutter. Those dark eyes. That stubble-dotted movie-star jawline. He's so different from Griffin, who had an all-American wide-eyed baby face, and whose best attempt at a beard was a few downy platinum whiskers. This guy could be a serial killer, yet my ticker is still screaming, "Bring it on!"

I'm not sure how long I stare at him, openmouthed, but the next thing I know, he reaches down and begins to pat my shin with a napkin. I have no idea how I miss the ceiling, because I jump like I'm on a trampoline. I look over the tie of my apron; the blood is trickling down to my pink Crocs. I snatch the napkin from him and back away.

"I'm sorry," he says. "You should get that looked at."

I ignore him; it's nothing a good Band-Aid won't fix. "How did you know I worked here?"

He shrugs. "Oh. I didn't. The owner told me that one of his employees would be spending the summer away, so he needed the help. Is that you?"

"Um . . ." I am about to say yes, but I'm afraid if I do, this guy will show up in New York, too. "Maybe?"

He nods, as if I make any sense, and puts his hand under my elbow. "You should sit." At first I want to say, *Get away,* but then I feel the blood seeping under my heel. With his help, I limp to a bench and collapse onto it. He inspects the gash. "You might need medical attention."

"I'm fine." I crane my neck toward Gyro Hut. I haven't spoken to Bret since last night, and I don't want to. Ever.

"He's not there," the guy says gently, still dabbing at my wound. With every dab, a new goose pimple appears. I realize that they're multiplying like rabbits. And that my leg has all these blue veins in it. Great, a hot guy is playing nurse to me, even if he is a stalker, and I have skin better suited to poultry.

"Who?"

"Bret. Your friend."

Okay. Back up now. "Wait. How did you know that he . . ."

He pauses for a moment, looking flustered. "I'm sorry. I'm frightening you. That's not my intention. Bret . . . overslept, so he will not be in today."

I squint at him. "And you know that because . . ."

"He, uh, nine-one-oned the shop a moment ago."

Is he speaking English? Or is that new Canadian slang? "Huh?"

The guy's hands twitch and his olive cheeks take on a rosy sheen. It has the effect that puppies in a pet store window have on me; I fight the urge to scoop him up and say, "Aw!" Finally, he stutters, "Um, t-telephoned? The shop. He asked me to l-let you know, in case you were looking for him."

"Oh," I say, relaxing. Like I would be looking for him now. And why did he bother calling the ice cream shop when he could have just called my cell? I reach into my pocket and pull out my cell phone, but there are no messages, no missed calls. Something sounds fishy, but I can't bother thinking about it, because a couple of preteen girls wearing way too much makeup are in the Sweetie Pi's queue. "Customers."

I struggle to my feet but he holds out his finger, then hurries behind the counter, saying, "How may I help you?" to the giggling schoolgirls like he's done this all his life. My bleeding has slowed, so I stand up and make my way toward the storefront. I hear the soft-serve machine purring; then the cash register dings, and the girls stroll away, licking their cones. When I arrive behind the counter, he's fishing an errant Swedish Fish out of the rainbow-sprinkle tray with a plastic spoon. "So . . . been an ice cream scooper before, have you?"

He shakes his head. "I have visited a soda fountain, though, many a time. I'm quite fond of sweet treats."

Soda fountain? Maybe that's what they still call these places where he's from. Someplace in . . . Canada, or so he said. Is it possible for there to be a place up north where they're that closed off from the world? Maybe they're like the Amish. I wonder if they still ride in horse-drawn carriages and use outhouses. "Listen," I say. "I do want to thank you for your help last night. But you may have gotten the wrong idea. Bret wouldn't have hurt me. He's been a—"

"Friend for a long time," he finishes, nodding. "I understand that's how you feel. But people you know, even very well, can surprise you."

"Maybe. How did you know where to find me, anyway?"

He shrugs, then reaches over and grabs a cup. "Do you think the management would object much if I . . ."

"Knock yourself out."

"Would you like anything?"

An hour ago, my mom made me her famous graduation pancakes, complete with a whipped cream smiley face and strawberry sauce, which she does the morning after every school year ends. My stomach is already pressing against the waistband of my shorts. "No thanks."

He gets to work, busily compiling ingredients, and I can't help wondering how he can be so proficient at this on his very first day. Finally, he pours chocolate syrup over a frothy mixture in the Styrofoam cup, then slides a straw into it and takes a sip. "Ah. Haven't had one of these in ages."

I stare at him. "Did you just make an egg cream?"

He nods. "Is there a problem?"

"No, I . . ." Suddenly, I feel tingles everywhere, and not the good kind. "It's just not exactly a very popular menu item."

"Is that so?" He takes another sip and swallows, punctuating it with an exaggerated "Ah!" "I've just . . . had an inexplicable craving for one in the last day or so. I quite enjoy them."

After that, the conversation lags. I end up staring awkwardly at the giant rotating light-up cone in the corner while he inspects the flooring. Finally, I say, "What did you say your name was, again? Aaron?"

"Eron. Eron DeMarchelle."

"Eron? Is that short for something?"

He nods. "Geronimo."

"Eek. No wonder you go by Eron. Are you named after a relative?"

He shakes his head. "It's a very popular name in Italy. I was born there."

"Italy?"

"Yes. Mama and I moved here when I was five. I mean, to, um, Canada. And then I moved here a few weeks ago. It was quite a bit different, where I came from."

"Oh." No duh. Based on his weird dress and stiff way of talking, he could be from Mars. Maybe his mom is adamant that he not stray too far away from the customs of his homeland. My mom always insists on bringing out her record of goofy Polish folk songs whenever we have company. I can't think of anything else to ask, so I say, "DeMarchelle sounds French."

He nods. "It is. My stepfather was."

"Was?"

"Oh, yes. He's passed. Mama, too."

"Oh." I can't say he seems very upset by it, but I add, "I'm sorry."

"It was a long time ago."

Time. That's it. He's not acting like he's from another place; he's acting like he's from another time. Another *century.* I look down at my feet, his feet. I point at his spats. "I didn't realize that those things were making a comeback."

He smiles at me. "They're quite comfortable. And, Julia, I'm sorry if I gave you reason to be suspicious of me."

"I'm not suspicious." Crazily uncomfortable, yes. Suspicious, no. Well, maybe a little. Okay, I'm so suspicious I'm practically itching.

"You don't seem the type to ask just anyone his life story."

I blush, then cross my arms. "Well, sorry. But you've just *coincidentally* shown up in my life three times in the past couple of days, first saying you have a message for me, then saying you want to protect me. You don't even know me. And then you go and order Griffin's favorite drink, so I'm just freaking out a little here." I realize I'm babbling and clamp my mouth closed.

He doesn't speak for a moment. Then he says, "I'm sorry, but I do understand. I see how it would all seem rather coincidental, but that is all it is. Even the fact that your beloved and I share an affinity for egg creams."

I look up. "My . . . *beloved?*"

I spend the rest of my five-hour shift trying to convince myself that everything about Eron DeMarchelle is normal, that anything wrong with him is just a product of my overactive imagination, much like those feelings that Griffin is haunting me are.

Though even my overactive imagination can't seem to figure out how this guy knew that Griffin was my boyfriend. Er, *beloved*. Whatever.

Since the mall is like a morgue again, I can't throw myself into my work. So I stack cups. This time, I make a sort of Eiffel Tower. Eron hums around like a busy bee, cleaning every surface with a wet rag. Then he finds a mop and bucket in the back. The floor of Sweetie Pi's is so sticky it probably hasn't seen that mop in a decade. Then he gets on a ladder and starts to clean a year's worth of dust from the top of the freezer. He's, like, Robo-Employee.

After the Eiffel Tower has collapsed, I sit down and start to yawn, just watching him. "You are making me look bad," I mutter.

He smiles as he wrings out a rag in the sink. "It's been quite a while since I've worked so hard I could feel it in my bones. I enjoy that feeling. Makes me feel . . . alive."

I notice he's blushing again. "Ooohkay," I say, thinking that if I worked that hard, the last thing I'd be feeling is alive.

At the end of the shift, he helps me untie my apron. His fingers tickle the back of my neck. I shiver as he slides the apron from my body and folds it neatly, but I blame it on the air-conditioning and the chocolate milk shake I just slurped down. When he walks me outside to my mom's car, we don't speak much. I don't have anything to say to him that isn't a question, and I know I've asked more than the polite share of those.

He holds the mall door open, and just as I'm thinking, Oh, how sweet, he extends the crook of his elbow to me. I stand there for a moment, wondering if he's just trying to check the time on his wristwatch, but then I realize he isn't wearing one.

Tentatively, I put my hand on his forearm, and he clasps his hand over it, just like in those old-time movies. We're *strolling*. People stare at us. My heart starts to thud madly under my camisole when he turns and smiles at me. "It has been a pleasure, Julia," he says, taking my hand in his. I know it's all sticky with chocolate syrup, but he doesn't seem to mind. Those eyes never leaving mine, he bends slightly and delivers a kiss to the top of my hand.

CHAPTER 20
Eron

Mama used to have a saying: "You get what you get." I'll admit she wasn't the most poetic of women, but at the time, she was raising eight children who weren't her own while barely able to speak their language. I think that was the first full sentence she learned to say in English, because the DeMarchelle children were always asking for more. More pasta, more space on the mattress, more everything. She'd curse at them in Italian, her native language, and then at my father, for dying and leaving her alone, and then she'd just smile at me and slip me an extra slice of warm *pane*.

It's been almost a hundred years and I can still taste that bread, feel it toasting up my palms. It was one of the few things that made life in the DeMarchelle household happy.

I'd come to Ellis Island with little more than my name, Geronimo Bianco, and then I lost even that, not two days after we'd set foot on American soil. Mr. DeMarchelle, my stepfather, helped Mama make the arrangements for Papa's casket, and probably pretended to be charming and gentlemanly only because Mama was a handsome woman and he could see a great opportunity. After all, he was recently widowed and had more children than he knew what to do with. And Mama couldn't speak a lick of English; she'd expected that Papa would handle all that. When Mr. DeMarchelle took her in front of a judge a day later, she was thinking it was just another step toward becoming an American citizen. She didn't expect to become Maria DeMarchelle, any more than I expected to become Eron DeMarchelle.

What other choice was there? My father had been the man with the plans, the aspirations to move to America and start his own business. Mama had wanted to stay back home with her family.

"You get what you get," I mutter under my breath, wringing out my one and only undershirt in a sink coated with dried toothpaste and pink mildew. Luckily, it is a warm night. I spread the material out, next to my undershorts and shirt, on an old towel in the window, hoping the night air will dry them by tomorrow.

Tomorrow, when I continue to make a fool of myself at the soda fountain.

I sigh, thinking of Julia. I've barely spent more than ten hours with her, and she's already suspicious of me. I'd expected not to fit in right away, but I hadn't anticipated that the truth would be exposed in mere days.

I pull the pair of shorts Harmon lent me over my hips; they're much too big, but they'll have to do for now. I'm thankful to have *something* to wear while my only outfit is laundered. At the very least, I'm grateful I can stay inside, as this attire certainly isn't suitable for the street. I went a hundred years without laundering that suit; Sandmen don't have to worry about such things, so I almost forgot how quickly the human world could wear on a piece of clothing. Though I'm still human only half the time, the suit is already dingy. The ice cream shop won't pay me until Friday, and most of Harmon's clothing is ill-fitting rags, so I have no other choice.

You get what you get.

I sink into the beaten couch, remembering my first days in the DeMarchelle home. In truth, Harmon's home is heaven compared to where I once lived on earth. The couch is lumpy and old, yes, but it will be pleasant compared to wrestling on a stained mattress with the eight DeMarchelle *demoniettos*, as Mama called them. There were Alfred, the eldest, and Clementine, the youngest, who was nearly my age, and in between, a gaggle of others who hated Mama for moving in and replacing their dead mother. Since I was her only son, they hated me, and because I was younger than all of them, I was an easy target. Not a day would go by when I wasn't nursing one bruise or another. I lean my head back on my arm, staring up at the ceiling fan. Paradise, no, but things could be worse.

I'm startled from my reverie when I hear glass crashing to the floor of the kitchen. It's Mr. Harmon; from the little I know of him, I have been able to determine that he always leaves a trail of wreckage in his wake. He stumbles into the doorway and stands there, a disheveled heap, holding a beer bottle to his lips. "Look who it is. My *guest*." The voice is dripping with sarcasm; "uninvited guest" is what he wanted to say.

"Hello," I say as cordially as I can. I sit up. "I've gotten a job. I should be able to help with your rent this month."

He wipes his mouth with the back of his hand. "Oh yeah?" He catches a glimpse of the apron I set out on the back of the sofa. "Serving ice cream?"

I nod.

He breaks into laughter.

"Is something funny?"

"You used to spend the night in the bedrooms of beautiful women. That was your *job*. Dishing out rocky road for snot-nosed kids is a *real* step up."

"It's a human job," I counter.

"And what about being human is so great?" he asks, shaking his head. "Look around you. Everyone you loved, everyone who ever loved you . . . they're fertilizer."

I'm not interested in listening to this drunk fool's rantings. It's true that Julia regarded me with caution during most of our time together this afternoon, but eventually, she . . . and others . . . will warm to me. Eventually, I will become one of them. "Yes, but in time . . ."

He laughs again. "You go back upstairs and ask an Original how many of us humans actually *make it* once we return to earth. How many go on to be happy, have good lives."

"Why don't you just tell me?" I say, prompting him, since it is obvious he is itching to.

He shrugs. "Okay. Nobody. We all end up either killing ourselves or drinking ourselves to oblivion or spending the rest of our days wanting death. That's a little secret the Originals don't let you in on when they ask you to join them. If humans knew the odds, trust me, they'd rather die."

"That's ridiculous," I say, though as I sit here, I realize I don't have any facts to base that opinion on. "We're all put here to complete our unfinished business."

He howls again with laughter. "Unfinished business? Oh, right. They're still feeding Sandmen that line of bull?"

I don't know how to answer. I don't know any other former Sandmen. I feel a twinge in the muscles of my back.

He takes another swig from his bottle; his dirty bathrobe falls open. "You're fading again."

I inspect my hands. So I am. At that moment, I remember I'm clad only in shorts. As I'm trying to slide my undershirt over my head—it's still quite damp—it slips through my fingers and I know I am once again a Sandman. I see Harmon speaking to the air—"Have a nice trip"—but I know he can no longer see me. I pass through the door, out to the street. Red and blue lights are flashing across the street, and a crowd is gathering there, but I don't stop. I am too busy regarding with disdain my bare chest and legs in the moonlight. I didn't expect this. How shameful it will be to confront Chimere half naked like this. But I must. She will say that Harmon is a fool, and I will have no choice but to believe her, but I must confront her.

I've never climbed the tree outside Julia's house barefoot. The branches scrape my legs as I climb to where Mr. Colburn is resting. "Where is Chimere?" I ask him.

He turns and grins at me. "Forgetting something?"

"I changed back into a Sandman while I was in the middle of dressing," I grumble. "Where is Chimere?"

He shrugs. "She was looking for you, too."

"She was?" Frustrated, I wave him off. No doubt she's

upset about how I interfered with Mr. Anderson. I press my bare back against the trunk of the tree and turn to the open window. It's dark; Julia has not yet returned home.

"So you gave Bret what he had coming to him?"

I nod and whisper, "Indeed I did."

I'm watching the darkened window, wondering what Chimere's punishment will be for me. Wondering if what Harmon said is the truth. Wondering when the inevitable question will escape Mr. Colburn's lips. It comes not a moment later: "So he's dead?"

I shake my head. "He is very much alive."

His face falls. "But you said—"

"I said I would take care of it. Bret Anderson is not the monster you make him out to be. Nothing about him even comes close to that creature that nearly murdered Julia when she was a child. Yes, his dreams may be somewhat inappropriate, but he's just a normal, hot-blooded boy, who *loves* her." I clench my fists. "It is not criminal to want her, but it is criminal for you to stand in the way by ending his life."

I can see the heat simmering under his white collar. "You want me to tell the elders—"

"I do not, but would you really hurt Chimere that way? Your mentor? You are not so cold."

He chews on his bottom lip. "If Bret so much as—"

"He will not. I assure you."

He sighs, opens his mouth, but closes it a moment later. For the first time since I met him, he has been silenced.

I walk away then, without another word. Triumphant. Perhaps my student can be taught after all.

CHAPTER 21
Julia

Hart Avenue isn't exactly the kind of place where you'd want to hang out after hours. Actually, I don't think I'd want to hang out here before or during hours, either.

But then again, I'm not really sure what I'm thinking.

"Hon," my mom says as we pass a bag lady meandering down the street with a shopping cart filled with trash bags for the fifteenth time. "What are we doing?"

"Uh," I say, trying to remember the excuse I came up with during my Sweetie Pi's shift. "This is a good street to practice parallel parking on."

And really, it is. It's one of the few streets in town with parallel parking and meters; plus there are so many cars and people and garbage cans and other obstacles everywhere that I imagine if I can park my mom's RAV4 here, I'll be able to park anywhere.

"Oh," she says. I make a turn and head down the next street, preparing to go around the block and cruise down Hart again. Just as I'm beginning to think she bought the excuse, she says, "But why do I feel like we're casing the joint?"

I wonder what mobster movie my lily-white mom got that saying from and shrug. "I'm looking for a parking space."

"We passed a bunch." We turn onto Hart again, and she points out the window. "What about that one?"

"Um, too narrow."

We pass another. "And that one?"

"Those cars I'd be parking between are black! It's too hard to see them in the dark."

"Hon, are you nervous? Don't be. Parallel parking is simple."

I'm not, really—about that, anyway. My dad has put the cones on the street outside our house so often that I could probably park anywhere in my sleep. I'm as ready as I'll ever be for my driver's test in a couple of days. But I wanted to find out more about Mr. Geronimo DeMarchelle. Even though I'm positive I would remember a guy like him if I'd ever met him before, I still have the strangest sense of déjà vu around him, like we not only knew each other once before . . . but we knew each other *well*. And there were things that didn't add up. How did he know where to find Bret and me that night at the party? How did he know that Griffin was my boyfriend? That's why I performed a dozen games of twenty questions on him, trying to knock something loose from his past, some common bond. But there was nothing. Our lives are so different that he might as well have arrived in a time machine. So when he walked me to my mother's car at the end of our shift, I couldn't help wanting to know more.

The kicker came right before we parted, when he kissed

my hand. After that, he nodded respectfully to my mother, placed his hat on his head, and sauntered away, whistling. He put the hat on like it was something he'd done every day of his life. Griffin would have done something like that as a joke, as part of an act, and would have looked utterly ridiculous. But Eron seemed comfortable with it, and when he kissed my hand, his eyes bored into me so that immediately my wrist went limp. Then shivers traveled up my arm, down my body to my knees, so I had to grab on to the car door to stop from toppling over on the curb.

And now, even though all that happened nearly an hour ago, I can still feel the imprint of his lips on my hand. Griffin used to kiss me deeply on the mouth, like they do in the movies, and I never felt as much. Okay, I felt more than with Bret, yes. Maybe a quickening of the pulse, a little fire. Sometimes it wouldn't even feel all that wonderful, like something was nibbling off little pieces of my flesh. Griffin was the first guy I'd ever kissed, so I assumed it would always be like that, with anyone. So now all I can think of is what it would be like to kiss a guy who could practically set my hand ablaze with a G-rated, gentlemanly gesture. I'm the Ice Princess. Things like that can't happen to me.

I search the street again and there's no sign of a guy in spats and a white dress shirt. This is ridiculous, anyway. What would I say to him if I saw him? *Hey, you forgot your apron.* It's not like I can test out my kissing theories on him in the middle of the street, surrounded by a bunch of drug dealers and homeless people, while my mom waits in the car. This plan has failure written all over it. And he said he'd be working at Sweetie Pi's tomorrow, so I am not sure why I have this burning feeling that if I don't see him right now, I'll go crazy.

There's a guy walking down the street, and though he's too short and his white bald head shines in the streetlight, I slam on the brakes beside him. A car horn blares behind me. My mom grabs the door handle for support. I catch a glimpse of myself in the side mirror. I look like a madwoman. Like I'm obsessed. And over what? What I really need right now is to go home and get some sleep.

Sighing, I slow in front of a parking space I saw the past three times we drove by. "I guess I'll just do this one," I say. I line my front bumper up with the parked minivan's front bumper and throw the car into reverse. Then I check my rearview mirror, turn the wheel all the way to the right, and slowly back into the parking spot.

As I'm straightening the wheel, my mom beams at me. "Bravo!" she says, clapping. "I don't think I could have done any better."

She opens the car door to check and I can see the curb—six inches. It's perfect. "Thanks," I mutter, too embarrassed with myself to properly celebrate the victory. I check my rearview mirror again to make sure no traffic is coming before I pull out.

And there he is.

In a picture window across the street is Eron's figure, framed in light. His back is to me but I can tell by the shock of black hair, now a little messed, and the well-defined curve of his back. He's in one of the shabbier buildings on the street, standing on a second-floor landing, spreading out laundry. He's . . . he's . . . *not wearing any clothes!* Before all the air can be pushed out of my lungs, before I can have a coronary, I blink a few times and focus. No . . . at that moment, he hikes up a pair of gym shorts that have fallen dangerously below his thin waist. He brushes the dark hair out of his eyes and turns his broad back toward the window, then sinks out of view. I sit there for a moment, quietly willing him to come back, and then I remember my mom.

Now she has both feet pressed down on the floor mat and is biting her lip as she watches a couple of lowlifes leering on a stoop near us. "Ready to go whenever you are," she says, but I know she's thinking, Now, please?

"Um. Oh. Okay." I glance up at the window again as I shift the car into drive. It's not like I can throw stones up at his window and say, *Yoo-hoo! I was just in the neighborhood!* anyway.

Eron turns back toward the street, and now there's a worried look on his face. He picks a T-shirt up, shakes it out as if he's about to put it on, and then . . .

Then . . .

He disappears.

I'm vaguely aware my jaw has fallen into my lap. The white material of his shirt—the material that only two seconds ago was in his hands—floats peacefully in the air and settles somewhere out of view. Okay, no. That didn't just happen. He must have fallen, or jumped away, or something. He couldn't have . . . There's no way . . .

"Let's get a move on!" my mom urges in her most commanding voice, startling me.

I spring upright, forgetting I've already put the car into drive, and press on the accelerator.

And barrel straight into the minivan parked ahead of us.

CHAPTER 22
Eron

Shortly after ten this morning, I become human again and rush to the apartment on Hart Avenue in my bare feet, hoping not too many people will see my shameful nakedness. When I climb the stairs and open the door to the living room, I groan. The room smells even more like rotting garbage than it did yesterday. Worse, Harmon, that drunken fool, has thrown all my clothes into a messy pile in the corner, and a partly bald yellow cat is lounging in it, licking its paws.

I shoo the cat away and shake out my trousers, balking at the dreadful stench. If I put these on, I will smell like a dying animal for the remainder of the day.

The doorbell rings, and I'm still attempting to determine if any of my clothing can be salvaged when I fling open the door.

I stop shaking out my shirt and stare.

It's Julia.

"How . . . how did you know where I live?" I ask, my body still frozen.

"You told me," she says.

We stand there for a moment, awkwardly, until I remember

simultaneously that I'm nearly naked and that I am not being a very good host. "Where are my manners? Please come in," I say, throwing my cat-hair-covered button-down shirt on and motioning to my sleeping couch. There are a few dirty dishes and cereal bowls there. I quickly scoop them up, spilling sour milk on my shirt. Perfect.

Julia looks around unsurely, wrinkling her nose, then sits on the couch. Her long legs are bare. She has a large flesh-colored bandage over the wound she got yesterday, but it looks much darker, almost brown, against her pale skin. "You live here?" She seems shocked, but no more surprised than I was when I walked in.

I nod. "Would you like something to drink?" I ask. I am relieved when she shakes her head. From what I've seen, I don't think Harmon would be too pleased parting with his beloved ale, and I know it's not Julia's drink of choice. I turn in time to see her gaze move abruptly away from my collarbone. There is still a rather jagged red scar there, where the machine at the textile mill wrenched my arm apart from it. She doesn't seem any more disgusted by it than she does by her surroundings, but still, I feel myself blushing like a schoolgirl. "Is there something I can help you with?"

"You said you had the noon shift at Sweetie Pi's. So do I. I was hoping you could give me a ride?" She smiles sheepishly, and it is so endearing I would say yes in a heartbeat, if only . . . "I would have called but I didn't have your number."

"Um . . ." I watch a large cockroach scuttle across the floor, near her delicate toes. She doesn't notice. "I don't . . . do that."

"You don't do what?"

"I don't have a . . . vehicle," I answer.

"You take the bus or something?"

"No, I walk."

"Walk? It's like five miles."

She says it as if the moon is easier to reach, as if walking is not something that's done anymore. "I . . . like the exercise."

"Oh. I'll walk with you."

I survey the shambles that was my quality suit—the herringbone jacket, the fine suspenders—which the cat is now chewing on. I wonder how many customers I will scare away in that. How long it will be until Julia is also frightened away. If only I'd never told her where I lived! I pull the shirt tightly across my chest. "Of course," I say hesitantly. "Let me just find some suitable attire."

She shrugs and I head down the hallway, hoping that Harmon has something that will fit me other than the horrid rags he offered earlier, something that won't be too disgraceful. I can hear him snoring before I push open the door. When I do, I rifle through his drawers quietly. They're mostly empty, because much of their contents are lying in soiled piles on the ground. In the closet, I find a pair of denim jeans like I used to wear in the textile mill, a belt, and a white shirt that isn't too wrinkled. I dress quickly in the hallway. The jeans are the wrong size, a little too short and a little too loose, but the belt helps. I tuck the shirt in, splash some water on my face, and sigh. For the first time in a hundred years, I need a shave, but I do not have a razor. And since I can't find one in Harmon's mess, and I'd rather not leave Julia to do battle with the cockroaches any longer than I have to, I step into my dress shoes and hurry to her. "I'm ready," I say, rubbing my chin as if that will help erase the awful stubble from it.

If my presentation is inadequate, she doesn't seem to notice. I think she was more questioning when I was wearing my fine suit. Perhaps she is in too much shock from the filthy apartment, too eager to escape it, because she stands and follows me out the door, clinging closely to my heels. We walk outside and down the front stairs, to the street. I say, "I'm sorry about the apartment. I haven't had the time to — "

Immediately she says, "Oh, no, that's okay. I hope you weren't upset by me coming over. I just wanted to see if I could bum a ride because . . . my mom's car had a little accident."

"Oh? I hope nobody was hurt," I murmur.

She shakes her head. We walk in silence a little more and then she says, "Actually, that wasn't the reason I came over."

"Oh?" I repeat, staring at the ground. Because I already know from her incessant questioning yesterday why she came to my home. She's still suspicious. And who's to blame her? I play the part of a modern youth sorely.

"Tell me how you know so much about me," she says. Out of the corner of my eye, I see her looking straight ahead, face tense.

"I'm sure I don't know what you mean."

"You know so much more about me than any stranger would. That's what you're supposed to be, right? A stranger. But you're not."

I force a laugh. "Julia, I'm not sure what you're suggesting, but — "

"There's something really weird going on. And you're part of it." She takes a deep breath. "I've met you before, haven't I?"

"No." But I'm not very good at lying. "Not exactly."

"Did you know Griffin?"

I nod a little.

"From . . . ?"

She whirls around and brings her eyes to meet mine. I swallow. If she holds my gaze for much longer, I know I will tell her everything. I break eye contact quickly. "He is . . . *was*, I mean, an acquaintance."

Of course I can see the puzzlement on her face. She brings her hair forward, over her ear, to cover her scars, suddenly self-conscious. "That message you had. Asking me to be careful. I've been trying to figure out who could have sent it, because other than my parents, nobody else would care that much about me. It was from Griffin, right?"

"Yes."

"He gave you a message because he wanted to protect me? But why . . . unless he knew he was going to die?" She stops. Her eyes widen. "Wait . . . when did he give you that message?"

I know she is putting the pieces together, and all I can do is stand there and watch the curtain I've placed between us unravel. "Julia, I . . . ," I begin, but I don't know what else to say.

"He died weeks ago, but strange things have been happening since then. Things that make me feel like he's still here." She taps on her temple. "I know it's crazy."

I watch her silently, trying not to leak anything, but I know it isn't working.

She gasps. "So it's true. He gave you that message *after* he died, didn't he?"

CHAPTER 23
Julia

"Julia . . . ," he says, looking away.

Okay. Did I just say that aloud? That I think my dead boyfriend is contacting me from beyond the grave, and Eron is the conduit? Way to win friends and influence people. "Um, forget I ever said anything," I say lamely, noticing a storm drain that I would love to climb into.

"I don't think you're crazy, Julia," he says after a moment.

Well, sure he doesn't . . . yet. He doesn't know that I could have sworn I saw him disappear into thin air last night. "Really?"

"Really." He says it like he means it. Griffin would have been on to insult number twelve by now.

"Who are you?" I ask softly. "Are you someone who can communicate with the dead? Have you been speaking with—"

He extends his hand as

if to say, *Hold it there, little lady.* He's obviously trying to calm me, because I can feel the heat swirling in my face and the pounding in my temples, as if there's a storm inside me raging to get out. "No, nothing like that."

I look down at the olive skin of his hand. There's something all too familiar about the way he holds his hand above my shoulder so that it's almost, but not quite, touching my skin. "Why do I feel like I've known you longer than just three days?"

"It's not important who I am," he says. "The important thing is that you—"

"Stay safe," I say, rolling my eyes. "I have parents who warn me about that every day. Why *you?*"

He doesn't answer my question, just stands there, fidgeting from one foot to the other. It's odd that at times he seems so mature, beyond-his-years mature, yet sometimes, he's almost like a little boy.

"Where did you get that scar? On your shoulder?"

He shakes his head. "No matter. It was a long time ago."

I know that they're obvious, that he's probably seen them before, but I lift the hair from my cheek and tilt my chin into the sunlight. I'm not sure why I want to tell him now, but I'm not sure of so many things when it comes to him. Maybe it's because I'll go mad if I don't get answers from him now. "I'll tell you my story if you tell me yours," I whisper.

"You don't have to say a thing," he says, gently taking my hand away from my cheek. It's as if he already knows how difficult it would be to tell. As if he already knows everything anyway. He says, "Your beloved . . . Griffin. Did you trust him?"

"Yeah," I say immediately, but the second the word leaves my lips, my resolve weakens. "I mean, I guess. We had a weird relationship."

"Weird?"

"Well, he liked to joke a lot. He'd laugh at a funeral. Nothing was ever serious to him. But he was a good guy."

"And he loved you."

"Yes. Well. We never said so, in so many words."

He smiles. "It only takes three."

"No, you see . . . we didn't talk about anything serious. Ever. And I kind of liked that."

He looks puzzled. "You did?"

"Well, yeah. I'm . . . Something happened to me when I was a kid. And afterward, everyone walked on eggshells around me. But Griffin didn't. We never talked about serious stuff like that. He treated me like anyone else. Which was good."

I bite my tongue. There I go again, spilling my soul to him, as if we're old friends and didn't just meet three days ago. Maybe it's because I'd never have been caught having this kind of serious discussion with Griffin and I'm starved for a heart-to-heart. Pathetic. I can just imagine Griffin pretending to throw a rope around his neck and hang himself. "And we were not really an emotional, lovey-dovey type of couple. Why am I telling you this? I need to shut up."

He laughs. "No, you don't. I like hearing you talk."

"Really?" I turn to him, and his face is serious as he nods. No indication that he's going to poke fun at me. "You really don't think I'm a nut job?"

He laughs. "Not at all."

"I like talking to you, too."

I'm just starting to feel better, like maybe I'm not completely losing it, when suddenly my flip-flop catches on an uneven piece of pavement and I fall forward. I land half in the grass, half on the sidewalk. My palms and my knees break my fall, but I scrape the left one of each on the pavement. Blushing, I roll over onto my backside, inspecting my bleeding body parts. While this is when Griffin and Bret would laugh and say, "Have a nice trip?" or something, Eron rushes to my side and pulls a handkerchief out of the pocket of his baggy jeans. Two thoughts hit me at once: First, what guy who isn't eighty years old carries a handkerchief? And secondly, is it possible ever to meet Eron without having an injury? Is there a reason I become a bumbling idiot around him?

My palm is just a little red and coated with gravel, so Eron brushes the grit away from my knee and clamps the cloth over it. It's not bleeding as much as the cut on my shin yesterday did, but now I have a wound on each of my legs. I look like I shaved with sandpaper. I'm going to make a great impression in New York.

The injuries sting, but suddenly there's a throbbing in my ankle. When he pulls me to my feet, that throbbing becomes a shooting pain. I howl.

"Is your ankle twisted?" he asks, settling me back down. He seems reluctant at first and blushes again, but eventually he gently places his fingers on either side of my ankle, moving upward. At one point, the pain is so bad I whimper.

"I think so," I say. "I am officially a moron."

He reaches down and picks me up. He hefts me into his arms easily, as if I'm just a bag of groceries. "I'm taking you home."

That sounds just fine to me. "But I live a mile away," I say, embarrassed.

"Not at all," he answers. It's a hot day, and his breathing isn't labored, so I relax a little, even though I still feel like a goober. "I just hope it is not broken."

"Let's not overreact," I say. "I'll be fine."

He carries me the entire way without so much as getting red in the face. I hand him my keys and he holds me up with one arm while opening the front door, then lifts me easily up the stairs. I'm about to direct him where to go, but he never hesitates; he steps to the right and twists open the door to my room, without a word. A weird sensation creeps over me as he lays me in my bed, lifts the sheets out from under me, and covers me. I'm only marginally aware of my hot-pink thong panties lying on the shag carpet, near his feet. How did he know which bedroom was mine?

"Thanks," I say, nonchalantly reaching down and sweeping the panties under my bed. That's when I notice my old Zac Efron poster, across the room, framed by my posters of the Eiffel Tower and Big Ben. I've been meaning to tear it down ever since I started dating Griffin, but now it hangs there, in all its glory, a testament to my lameness. Strangely, though, Eron seems to be focused completely on me.

"Not at all. I will telephone the management of the soda fountain and tell them of this unfortunate incident."

"You mean, you're not going in?"

He shakes his head. "And who would play nurse to you? I think you need to stay off that ankle."

"No, really, I'm fine. . . ."

He smiles. "I insist."

I settle back in the pillows. "You really don't have to."

"Julia . . . ," he says, wagging a finger at me to say, *Stop arguing.*

"Fine. Um, I think my mom has some soda in the fridge. No egg creams, unfortunately."

Eron laughs, his eyes never leaving mine. They're focused in such a way that makes me a little queasy. Or maybe that's just the heat. Or maybe it's that right then, I realize that Eron doesn't seem to take notice of his surroundings at all, as if he's not interested. Or as if he's already seen my bedroom a thousand times before.

"You're Italian, is that right?" my mom says, inspecting Eron as she ladles gazpacho into his bowl. A little of it spills onto the table.

He nods politely.

I hope Eron realizes what he's in for. My mom could make the most hardened of criminals weep. Add my father, and it's past cruel and unusual. If Eron thought my questioning was harsh, he may end up jumping from something very high at the end of this meal. That's why I only brought Griffin around my parents once. Only once.

My mom is smiling sweetly, but that's just one of her tactics: make them think she's on *their* side, then strike. "Do I know your parents?"

"Mom . . . ," I groan.

"They're . . . deceased, ma'am," he says.

She purses her lips. I wait for her to offer condolences but that would reveal she has a heart and shift the power into his court. "So where do you live?"

"With my brother. On Hart Avenue."

"Hart?" She turns to me and glares. I can read her mind: *So*

162

did he have anything to do with the $1,200 repair bill for the RAV4? I just smile sheepishly and shrug. "Are you in school?"

"Not any longer," he says.

"You've graduated?"

"I . . . left school, after eighth grade," he says. "I needed to find a job."

My dad nearly chokes on his soup. "But . . . school is very important!" he chimes in, like a public service announcement. My mom's eyes narrow in disgust. Normally she'd have pity for a guy whose parents were dead and who had to drop out of school to get a job, but because her only child brought him home to dinner, because he's a guy and *who knows what evil lurks in the hearts of men,* he's bad. I kick her under the table. She turns to me. I try to communicate telepathically: *You are not interrogating a terrorist. Stop with the third degree.*

She seems to get the picture, but then my dad starts in. "What are your plans for the future?"

"Dad," I mutter, scooping the soup into my spoon and letting it dribble back into my bowl. My mom is always trying random recipes she gets from various shady sources; this "gazpacho" idea came from the back of a can of lima beans and tastes like water. "Stop." I mean, questions about his future? Please. I see dinner in our future. And possibly me lunging across the table and gouging out my father's eyes with my spoon.

Eron smiles and wipes his mouth with a napkin. "I am interested in going back to school," he says, unwavering. He takes another sip of the soup. "I'd like to go back for architecture."

I stop trying to telekinetically murder my parents, and stare at him, forgetting I'm holding my spoon. It falls to the table with a

163

loud clatter. "Whoops," I say as green goo splashes across the table and onto the front of my hoodie. But come on, trying to butter me up by pretending to have the same interests as me? Please.

I take a napkin and start to wipe up the mess, and then I realize something. . . . Did I ever tell him that that was what I was going to major in at college? That I had dreams of designing buildings, too? I don't think I did. He just goes right on slurping his soup, not looking for a reaction from me. I think he's serious.

"Mrs. Devine, this soup is delicious," he says earnestly.

My dad and I both gape at him, then halfheartedly agree, just to be polite. The soup is good? For what? Considering that his apartment was littered with days of crusty old cereal bowls, I guess he isn't too much of a culinary expert himself.

My mom beams and doesn't say a word. I don't think anyone has complimented a meal of hers since before she was married. Even better, he asks for seconds. Eron has silenced the beast. Score.

Afterward, I hobble down the hallway and Eron sets me up on the couch, in front of the television. He lifts my foot and props a pillow under it. I get the feeling he's played nurse before, because his touch is gentle. Just like with the kiss last night, everywhere he touches begins to tremble. I hope he can't see what a bowl of Jell-O I am around him.

"Can I have the remote, please?" I ask him.

He tilts his head, looking perplexed. "The . . . ?"

"Remote," I say, pointing toward the television. It's sitting there, right on top of the entertainment center, plain as can be, and yet when he walks there, he fidgets for a moment, clearly unsure. Then he picks it up and hands it to me. "Thanks. Want to watch *House* with me?"

He purses his lips. "Watch the house? Is something going to happen to it?"

"You don't watch much TV, do you?"

The show starts. He shakes his head and sits down on the couch beside me. Instantly, he's enraptured. Some kid is having a convulsion on an airplane. Eron's eyes bulge. I can almost hear his heart beating, even from a cushion's length away. The kid flops around a little in the narrow aisle, white foam dribbling from his chin, and then it cuts to the opening credits. I don't think Eron has taken a breath since the show began. He turns to me. "That was . . . terrifying."

"But satisfying," I point out.

He nods and leans against the back of the sofa, making himself comfortable. "Will we find out what is plaguing that poor child?"

"Yep. At about eight-fifty-nine."

"Oh." He reaches into the pocket of his jeans and pulls out a long silver chain. I expect a wallet to be attached to it, but instead, he flips open this very elegant pocket watch and inspects it, then winds it a few times. "I probably should be going."

"Wow, that's cool," I say, reaching for it. He hands it to me and I turn it over in my hands. "My dad has one of these. It was his grandfather's. Who did this belong to?"

He shrugs. "It's mine. Mama bought it for me when I turned fifteen."

"Oh. I didn't know they still sold these. Cool." I inspect it, then awkwardly say, "I'm sorry about your parents. Seems like they were really cool."

He nods, sadness in his eyes. "Mama was a good woman. Papa died when I was five. My stepfather was . . ." He cringes. "Not a nice man."

"Oh," I say, not sure how to respond.

"He . . . killed my mother," he says.

My jaw drops. "What?"

"A long time ago. He was drinking," he mumbles. An awkward silence follows, during which I realize that that was why he was so filled with rage over Mr. Anderson's drunkenness at the party. A long time ago. His mother gave him the watch when he turned fifteen. He can't be more than eighteen now. Three years isn't really a long time when it comes to the death of a parent. Maybe he's just saying that to make things less awkward, like when I lie and say, "I'm fine," whenever anyone asks how I'm doing. A small smile creeps onto his face. "I'm sorry. I didn't mean to be so morbid."

I'm about to hand it back to him, but I stop when I notice something engraved in the cover. *Geronimo DeMarchelle, Happy Birthday, Love, Mama.* And the date, written out: *September thirteenth.* "Oh, wow, your birthday is the same as my parents' anniv—"

I stop. Because that's when I see the year. There's something off about it. At first I'm thinking, Okay, he got it in '08, not very long ago. But then it hits me. It's not 2008. It's . . .

He pries the watch quickly from my fingers and stuffs it back into his pocket.

"Can I see that again?" I motion for him to hand it over. He shuffles in his seat and suddenly becomes absorbed in a television commercial for dish detergent. "Did that say . . . 1908?"

He doesn't answer.

Okay, well, it's got to be a misprint. What other explanation could there be? "Why didn't you tell the engraver they screwed up?"

He looks at me. "I . . . I just didn't realize at the time."

"Oh. That sucks." Back on the television, House is ranting. I watch for a few minutes, then I remember. The weird outfit Eron was wearing when I first met him. The way he talks. The fact that a remote control is a foreign concept to him. *He acts like he just arrived in a time machine.*

Maybe it wasn't a misprint.

He turns to me. "Yes?"

It's only then that I realize I'm staring at him, my mouth half open. I clamp it shut and pull an afghan over the goose bumps on my arms. "Um. Just wondering if you would like some . . . um, Cheez-Its."

He wrinkles his nose. "Pardon?"

I gulp. Lack of Cheez-It recognition. Not a good sign. "Maybe some Oreos?"

I mean, everyone has to know Milk's Favorite Cookie, right? Not right. He's looking at me like I sprouted wings.

Oh, hell no.

What kind of thing is sitting on the couch with me? I throw the blanket off me and spring to my feet, intending to back away from him—far away. But I temporarily forget my twisted ankle, and when the pain shoots up my calf, I scream and fall forward, back toward the couch. Toward him.

He catches me. Steadies me in his lap. And doesn't let go. His eyes search my own as if there's something they're willing me to remember. Something about being here with him, this close, is all too familiar. It's like a scene from one of my recurring . . . dreams.

Dreams. That's it. "I dream of you," I murmur, dizzy, as everything seems to swirl around him. "All the time."

No, that's not it. That's crazy. How could you dream constantly of a guy you met only three days ago? My mind is still reeling when he leans down, his face just inches from mine, his hand stroking the scars on my cheek. And I don't feel the urge to cringe. He's going to kiss me, I know. And I want it to happen.

Badly.

I tilt my chin up to get there faster, and that's when he jolts forward, wincing. His eyes widen and he rubs the back of his head. I flash back to when Bret kissed me in the cafeteria; he had the same surprised, wounded expression. *Something hit me,* he said. But there's nothing behind Eron, nothing at all.

I can't help it: I think of Griffin. *You belong to me.*

"Are you okay?" I ask.

He nods quickly, then straightens and looks at his hands. He seems a little pale. He stands and helps position me back against the cushions. I'm wondering if I have bad gazpacho breath when he says, "I'm sorry, I must go."

"Oh . . . okay," I say, struggling to my feet. I want to ask, *What just happened here?* but I'm not really sure I'm prepared for the answer.

He holds up a hand. "I will let myself out. Good evening, Julia," he says, and exits so abruptly I shiver in the breeze he leaves behind him.

Good evening, I think. Who says that anymore?

CHAPTER 24
Eron

The sun slips behind the horizon as I step outside Julia's house. Just in time, for a few minutes later, Julia's face appears in her bedroom window. She's searching for me, eyes troubled, but does not see me. I'm a Sandman again. She must be wondering how I could have sprinted so far away from her front door so quickly.

I stop for a moment, breathing hard, and stare up at the stars, collecting myself. My body is shaking. Everything about being with Julia is like navigating shark-infested waters. I can't get as close as I've been used to for the past sixteen years because it's too close and I know that Mr. Colburn is watching. I cringe whenever she opens her mouth to ask me a question, as I can't talk about my past, my purpose, or many other things. I can't let her know that I know what she's thinking, that I understand. I'm supposed to be a stranger.

Maybe Harmon was right. Maybe it is impossible to fit in again.

I tread around the azalea bushes surrounding her house

and put my hands on the gnarled bark of that familiar oak. Before I can hoist myself to a branch, something topples on me from above. Something enormous, bearlike. I fall to the grass, gasping, but it is still on top of me, pressing against my mouth, grinding my head against the hard earth.

"What. The. Hell?" A voice whispers angrily into my ear.

Mr. Colburn. He pushes against my throat once more and then releases me. I sit up. "And a pleasant good evening to you," I snap.

His fists are clenched, his jaw tight. "What do you think you were doing?"

I shrug. "I don't know."

"You think I wouldn't notice you making a move for my girl?" he snarls.

I hold up my hands. "I was doing nothing of the sort. She slipped, and I was simply protecting her," I say, but even as I speak, I feel my face twitching. *You know it was more than that.*

Mr. Colburn senses my confusion. "Yeah. Right."

"I am trying my best."

He scowls. "You need to try a little harder. And here's a tip: don't lay a finger on her."

I rub the back of my head. "Seems you need to learn to keep your hands to yourself as well. What did I tell you about touching humans?"

"Stop giving me reason to," he growls just as the branch of a tree dips and Chimere appears. She lowers herself to the ground and steps gracefully and quietly between us.

"Children," she scolds, "Sandmen on the other side of the world can hear you."

Mr. Colburn's icy stare doesn't waver from mine. "He makes a sorry human."

"You make a sorry Sandman!" I retort, no longer caring if I do sound like a child. The nerve of him to suggest I am failing at my duties when he can barely follow the Sandman rules for a day.

Chimere smiles. "You two are both in a difficult transition period. You must be patient. Eron, Mr. Colburn is trying hard."

"He *hit* me. Again. When I was human."

"Oh, I'm sure it was just an accident. These things do happen. The training is right on schedule. Mr. Colburn just needs to control his impulses a little better." She takes his hand and pats it. "Isn't that right?"

He glares at me. "Yeah."

"Similarly, Eron needs to relearn proper human behavior. For a hundred years, he has had to move close to humans, nearly but not quite touching them, in order to affect them. He needs to reestablish normal human boundaries."

Reestablish human boundaries. Is that all? Then it is normal for a former Sandman to feel this conflicted? But why, then, do I feel conflicted only when I'm with Julia?

"And, Mr. Colburn," she continues, "it should not concern you how Eron spends his human days, anyway."

He spits on the grass. "He practically stuck his tongue down my girl's throat. Any idiot should know that's not a proper *human boundary.*"

"For the thousandth time, your *girl* is *not* your girl anymore!" I snap, knowing that Chimere will be behind me on this. After all, she was the one who convinced me, in my early years as a Sandman, that I needed to let my human attachments go. "Tell him, Chimere."

Instead, Chimere whirls to me, a peculiar, fragile expression on her face. Then she murmurs, not entirely convincingly, "That is right."

I can't do anything but marvel at her lack of authority.

She turns to Mr. Colburn and points up at Julia's bedroom window, which is dark. "Julia's been waiting for you for some time."

"Fine." He pulls himself up to the tree and jabs a finger at my chest. "If I see you *anywhere* in her dreams, you're dead."

I'm too busy studying Chimere to be alarmed by the threat. Chimere sighs. "What a character," she says, tittering, when he has passed out of earshot.

"You are too easy on him."

"What shall I do, my pet? Get out the paddle?"

"I recall," I say, "that when I was being trained, you held my feet to the flame for days if I so much as mentioned Gertie."

More tittering. "Perhaps I am softening in my old age."

"I think you've softened, but not because of age."

"What does that mean? I assure you, you are mistaken if you think I am favoring Mr. Colburn." She begins to braid her hair. "Perhaps you *are* jealous?"

I snort. "Ridiculous. Me? I just want to ensure that bumbling, pigheaded ass doesn't ruin us all. How could you tell him about what I did for Julia when she was seven? That was our secret. And now that he knows, nothing is safe."

She laughs again. She seems to enjoy seeing my feathers ruffled. "Calm yourself."

"How can I? You said yourself that the transition is difficult, and with him around, I'm always checking my back. I can't trust him. I'm constantly waiting for the other shoe to drop, for him to make some hideous misstep from which we can never recover." I run my hands through my hair and look up at the night sky. An airplane is streaking across it, red lights flashing. "The human I was placed with—Harmon. He told me human life after Sandman tenure is more than difficult. . . . He said it's horrid. Impossible. Is that the truth?"

Her eyes trail to the ground. She holds in a breath. "Harmon is a drunk. He was never the man you were."

I take her by her delicate shoulders and make her stare me in the eye. "Is it the truth?"

"You still have time, if you wish," she murmurs. Her reluctance to answer the question tells me everything I need to know.

"Chimere, what are you saying?"

"If you want to stay a Sandman, all you need to do is ask. You know I would love you to stay."

I slowly pry my fingers from her silken sleeves and sink to the ground, feeling more between worlds than ever.

I try to muster up the energy to feel excited about becoming human again, but it's impossible. Harmon is likely to give me a piece of his mind for stealing his clothes, and I'm more uncertain than ever about how I should behave around Julia. All her life I've done nothing but protect her, and now Mr. Colburn wants me to stay away, despite everything in my body telling me otherwise. Maybe I'm too much of a Sandman to be anything else. Though the thought of one day becoming human has occupied most of my mind for the past hundred years, suddenly, Chimere's words replay there as well: *If you want to stay a Sandman, all you need to do is ask.*

It's later in the morning, and I've been perched on the curb for some time, waiting to become human again. As the sun creeps to the top of the sky, I pull out my pocket watch. Nearly twelve. I should have changed by now.

Something is wrong.

Lately, whenever I've suspected something was wrong, I've immediately thought of Mr. Colburn. Did I even see him again after he crept into Julia's room to seduce her?

Oh, no.

I jump up and turn toward Julia's house. I can't recall seeing Julia leave. Surely she'd be up and about by now. Quickly, I scale the tree and peer inside, afraid of what I might see. But there's nothing to be alarmed by; Julia's bed is empty and neatly made, and she is gone. There is no sign of Mr. Colburn.

Relieved, I settle back in the tree, but am quickly startled by Chimere's face reflected in the window. Her hands are pooled in her lap, as if she can't decide what to do with them.

"Let me guess," I say.

"Last night. He never put his other charges to sleep." Chimere says these words as I'm thinking them. "He's vanished."

CHAPTER 25
Julia

My mom pulls this horrible orange and black blouse out from a rack and holds it against me. "Is this New York?"

My gaze travels out the window, into the parking lot, to the sun-speckled windshields of the cars. It's sunny and warm, yet my breath just about fogs up the glass, I'm panting so heavily. I can't stop it; I feel like I'm under a microscope. Being watched.

"Hello?"

I'm startled into reality. I scrunch my nose at her latest offering. "I don't think so."

"Hon, you've nixed every blouse in the store! Since when did you become so picky?"

"I'll look like a tiger. I think I should stay with safe colors. Black and gray."

Safe. Safe sounds really good right now. But what is safe? I'd thought my home, my bedroom, was safe. But last night, I dreamt of Griffin. He was so angry at me. And who could blame him? Instead of dreaming I was kissing Bret, I dreamt I was with Eron. But it was more than just making out this time. When I was with Bret, I'd pushed him away. In this dream, I was obviously having a kick-ass time. A small part of me knew I should stop, but the rest of me didn't want it to end. It was one of those dreams a person never wants to wake up from. And the next thing I knew, Eron was gone, and Griffin was standing over me, shouting, *You belong to me. Me!* He raised his hand, ready to strike, and then . . . I woke up, trembling and sweating all over my sheets.

And now I can't shake the feeling that he's here. That he saw me with Eron, with Bret. They both had painful spasms in the back of their heads when they got too close to me . . . so either there's a contagious brain tumor going around, or . . .

"Now, what fun are black and gray?" My mom crosses her arms and contemplates the shirt. I know she will beg me to try it on with hopes I'll fall madly in love with it once I feel the fabric on my skin, and I know I will cave. "Orange looks nice on you. And with your cute body, you should be saying, 'Hey, world, here I am!' "

I'm shocked. My mother has always hid me under her wing; she's never wanted the world to notice me. "No thanks," I mutter, reaching down to massage my ankle. At this point, I'd much rather blend.

"Oh, does it hurt bad?"

Not as much as my heart pounding against my chest like it's trying to escape. "Not so much. I just need to sit a second. Can we get a pretzel?"

We head outside the outlet and my mom buys a pretzel and a

lemonade from a stand on the sidewalk. She rips the pretzel in half and, as usual, gives me the bigger piece. Then we sit on a bench, our packages surrounding us. She's bought more than I have, though she doesn't really need anything. I have a pair of ballet flats, some skinny jeans, and a black pencil skirt. I can't decide whether the kids at the *Architectural Journal* will be going casual or businessy, so I've decided to pack a little of both. I should have plenty of purchases to show for our three hours at the outlets; after all, since my wardrobe is mostly shorts and flip-flops, I need just about everything. But I can't concentrate.

"Maybe we should just call it a day, shop some more when you're feeling better."

I'm glad I have my ankle to blame for my spaciness. "Yeah."

"I'd say you can drive home for the practice, but I don't know if that's a good idea."

I nod. Smart thinking. For once in my life, I am in no mood to drive.

"I hope you're feeling better for your big day tomorrow."

I stare blankly at her. Big day? Oh, she means my driver's test. How can it be that I've had that day circled in red on my calendar forever, but now that it's almost here, I'm a wreck? "Mom," I say. "Do you think I should postpone it?"

The shock is everywhere on her face. "Is this because of the accident?"

"Um . . . yeah," I say.

"Well, if you're in New York for the rest of the summer, I don't know when you'll be able to reschedule it." She studies me. "After all, the accident was just a symptom of the problem, wasn't it?"

It's uncanny the way my mom can read my mind. I nod.

"This is really about Griffin, right?"

I nod.

She puts her arm around my shoulder and pulls me so close that I can smell her Herbal Essences shampoo. "Oh, hon. I know you miss him. I know how much you loved him."

I blink. Okay, she shouldn't quit her day job to become a Psychic Friend just yet. How can she know how much I loved Griffin when even I don't anymore? How can I explain to her that it's not sorrow or grief I'm feeling . . . but guilt . . . and fear?

When we return home, I'm exhausted. All I want to do is trudge to bed, but the second we pull into the driveway, I see that's not going to be possible. Bret is standing on the front stoop, looking unsure, as if he doesn't know whether he should knock. He's never shown up at my house. In fact, I didn't know he knew where I lived. From the look on his face, I know why he's here. I cringe.

My mother eyes him like he's one of those door-to-door Holy Rollers come to lure me off to a cult. "Do you know this boy?"

I nod as she takes my one and only bag from me and opens the screen door, still shooting him eye daggers. "Yeah, Mom. It'll just be a second."

His smile looks about a second away from shattering into a thousand pieces. "So!" he says brightly as I sit down on the stoop beside him, but far away enough that he can't easily touch me. I can't bring myself to look at him, so I stare straight across the street, at two girls playing hopscotch on the sidewalk. "I found out who broke into my locker, I think. Someone on the track team. Anyway . . ."

"Oh yeah?" I say. I know he didn't come all the way over here to tell me that.

"Yeah." He is silent for a minute. I can tell he's going to open up a vein. And the last time he did that, he *kissed* me. That is not what I need right now, not after seeing Griffin in my dream. Not when I feel like he's here, watching. "Look, I don't really remember what happened that night. But I woke up feeling like scum, and knowing I should apologize to you."

I shrug. "Forget it." *Please.*

He laughs. "I did. I swear I can't remember a thing. But when you didn't call me these past couple of days, I knew you were angry at me."

"I'm not angry at you," I protest. "We're still *friends.*" I emphasize the last part, hoping he'll get the hint that this isn't an invitation to exchange bodily fluids.

"Right. Ippie, you're my best friend. And if that's what you want to stay, that's okay with me."

I heave a sigh and finally look at him. "Yes!" I say, maybe a little too enthusiastically. "Yes. Thank you. That's what I want to stay."

His face falls. I guess he didn't expect me to be so jumping-up-and-down excited about the proposition. "Okay," he says, standing. "Well, um. So we're okay?"

I nod. "Perfect."

"Good." He studies me. "You look a little beat. Shopping all day?"

"Yeah. I was. Um, getting clothes for New York."

"Oh. Right. Congratulations on that," he says, looking toward the street. "Call me later, okay?"

"Sure," I say, yawning and turning back to the house. I can't even feel glad that things between Bret and me are patched up. I'm too hazy, numb. I climb the stairs to my bedroom, pretty sure I'm already half asleep. After the second nightmare with Griffin, I spent most of the night awake in the dark, watching the shadows stretch across the ceiling. But now, as soon as I pull back the sheets and slide into bed, sleep overtakes me. In minutes I am dreaming.

Of Eron again.

He's standing on the street, staring up at the enormous buildings. The sky above and his skin take on the same grayish blue of the concrete. He's wearing his tuxedo, and when I come up behind him, he turns and I see that his tie and the first few buttons of his shirt are undone. "Good. You're here," he says.

"Where is here?" I ask.

"Don't you know? I've brought you here before. You're sleeping."

"Yes." I guess I did know that. For as long as I can remember, Eron has been the one to bring me to this place, which is why I've always felt safe with him. "Who are you?"

He doesn't answer; instead his face turns serious. "Have you seen Griffin here lately?"

"Yes. Last night. He was very angry at me."

Eron's hair whips in the breeze. "I was afraid of that."

"What does it mean?"

He moves close to me but does not touch me. He seems afraid to. Like he knows that that's the reason Griffin is so upset. He whispers, "If you ever see him in your dreams, you must do everything you can to awaken. Do you understand?"

"No, I don't. I—"

"He is much more powerful when you are asleep."

"Powerful? I don't understand . . ." My voice drifts off. "What is going on?"

I reach for him, but he steps away. The wind feels like ice on my skin. "I will do my best to protect you," he answers. He reaches over and pushes the hair out of my eyes, then strokes my cheek very gently.

Suddenly, storm clouds drift over us. He tilts his chin to them just as the first bolt of lightning slashes the sky.

"He's coming." He focuses on me, his eyes intense. "Wake up. Wake up, Julia."

I'm startled into reality. My curtains are flooding the room, carried by a fierce, whistling wind. Papers from my desk scatter to the floor. Everything in my room is cast in gray, the color of storm clouds. I lick my lips; despite the icy wind howling through the room, they're coated in sweat. I can't catch my breath.

I throw the covers off my body and race down the stairs.

CHAPTER 26
Eron

Despite my searching everywhere, Mr. Colburn is nowhere to be found. I suppose that wherever he is, he's more irritable than ever, since he shirked his regular duties. At times, while I stood over Julia, helping her take her afternoon nap, I sensed him near. I met Julia in her dreams and told her to beware; I knew he was there and furious that she'd been dreaming of me. It's early in the evening when I finally realize I'm human again. I'm not sure how long it will last, so I hurry to Julia's home. The moment I reach the front stoop, she swings open the front door, as if expecting me. Her gasp tells me that she wasn't, that she was just on her way out.

"I'm sorry to disturb —" I begin, but she quickly opens the screen door and ushers me inside.

"I was just going to find you," she says.

"You were?"

She nods. "I've been having these strange dreams. You were in them. And Griffin."

"Yes."

"I know it sounds crazy, but it's like he's here."

"You're not crazy, Julia. We can't find him. And I have no idea what he might do now."

"What he might . . . ?" she murmurs. "So you mean it's true? He's still here? Like a ghost?"

"No. But he is watching you. And he wants you to know he's there."

Julia sinks against a wall. "But why?"

"He's having a difficult time accepting the fact that he's no longer among the living. He wants everyone—and you especially—to acknowledge him."

She sniffs. "Sounds like something Griffin would do."

"Yes, it is a common problem among our kind."

She brings her eyes up to meet mine. They're glassy. "*Your* kind?"

I take a breath. We're forbidden to speak of the Sandmen to humans, and even though Chimere will probably scold me, Julia needs to know the trouble she is in. "Yes. We were all once human. But now we are"—I brace myself for her disbelief—"Sandmen."

"Sandmen?" She stares at me, eyes narrowing. "You mean, the men from the legends who put little kids to sleep?"

"We are not legends. We are very real."

She lets out a sour laugh. "Okay, where's your sand?"

I reach into my pocket. I still have some left from her afternoon nap. I sift a little through my fingers, letting it gather in my other hand. It sparkles, even in the minimal light, like pieces of crystal. She, predictably, yawns, as the sand has a powerful effect on humans, even when it does not come into contact with them. I stifle a yawn myself, the first one I've been challenged to suppress in a hundred years.

This fails to convince her. "I almost would have believed you if you'd said he was a ghost, but *this?* That's really out there. And if you're both Sandmen, why can I see you and not him?"

I rub the back of my neck. *Twinge.* Oh, not already. I shake my hands to free them of the sand and run them through my hair. "It's quite a long story."

"I have time," she says.

"Unfortunately, I do not," I say, reaching for the doorknob. "If you do not see me again today, I will see you tonight. In your dreams."

"But . . ." She jumps to her feet, readying to hold the door closed so I cannot escape, but then her eyes grow large and I know that she can no longer see me. She waves a hand where I stand, but it slips through me. Her mouth drops open. I want to hold her and tell her it's all right, but that's not possible. Perhaps it's better that she see my transformation; perhaps it will help her to believe the impossible. I pass through the door and into the dying sunlight.

Because, thanks to Mr. Colburn, my other charges didn't slumber at all last night, I decide to go to their houses first, well before their usual bedtimes. They'll undoubtedly want to turn in early. As I'm walking across Vicki's lawn, which is quite long and dotted with dandelions, I see Chimere sitting among the grass, blowing dandelion snow into the air. So carefree, despite our obvious problems, I think.

She smiles without looking up at me. "I made a wish for you, my pet."

"Thank you, my dear," I say, surveying the area. "So has Mr. Colburn returned?"

Her pert nose wrinkles. "He has been tending to his work only minimally, but never remains long enough for me to speak to him."

"Ah, the challenge."

Her smile broadens. "Yes, he is quite the fascinating one."

I kneel next to her. The grass is cold and wet on my knuckles. "I thought you would still be trying to capture him."

"When we do find him, we'll make sure he's dealt with accordingly," she says, tickling her nose with a dandelion.

"Accordingly? You mean the Last Place?"

"Perhaps. But you are here now, where you belong. I'd say all is right with the world."

I tilt my head. "Pardon?"

"You will be staying with us for the next hundred years, yes? I've already informed the elders and we are all so pleased."

I bristle at the suggestion. "I've said nothing of the sort, Chimere. It is only because Mr. Colburn has neglected his duties that I am now more a Sandman. But I firmly intend to become a human when my time arrives."

"Oh?" She sighs, as if she has just heard that rain is expected. "But your hundred-year anniversary is tomorrow. And without Griffin . . . Oh dear. I am afraid if he cannot assume his duties reliably before that time, we will have no choice but to keep you here."

"No choice?" Ire begins to bubble in my chest as I take in all she is saying. "But . . . then we must find him. What ever gave you the ridiculous idea that I wanted to remain here?"

"Well, Mr. Colburn indicated . . ."

"You believe him? After everything he's done?" I snarl.

She recoils, eyes wide. "But after our discussion, after everything Mr. Harmon has told you, I thought your choice would be obvious. . . ." Her eyes fill with such unexpected, unfamiliar rage, I'm forced to stand and back away. "Why do you always behave as though your life here is so torturous?"

"Harmon?" I watch as she seethes at me, her chest heaving underneath her pale blue corset. And that is when something dawns on me, something impossible. But obvious. "Originals study humans for years upon years, sizing up their personalities, before selecting one to be a Sandman. I often wondered why you chose Mr. Colburn as my student, as he is so stubborn, so unlike what you usually look for."

She takes an uneven breath, looks away.

"And if you wanted to *help* me, why did you place me with Harmon, a man who would undoubtedly show me the worst side of human life possible?"

"Eron, please—"

"You *wanted* me to fail, didn't you? You wanted me to stay here, forever."

"That's ridiculous," she mumbles, but there is no resolve in her voice.

"Is it, now?"

She tilts her face up to the moonlight and for the first time I see that her eyes are wet. "You have always been my favorite. My pet. I can't bear to imagine my existence without you."

I walk to her and unfold my handkerchief for her. Her cheeks are a flattering shade of red as I wipe the tears from them. Her eyes are still pooling with water as she watches me, then puts my arm around her delicate shoulders. "My dear, you would still have seen me in my dreams," I say.

"You'll never touch me or look me in the eyes again," she says, sniffing. "I suppose that's why I can't be too angry with Mr. Colburn. I understand when he says it's just not the same."

I know that my charges are waiting, but Chimere is my dearest friend, so she needs me, as well. I do nothing but hold her, there in the grass, for a long time, then watch her thread dandelions together to make a necklace. As I help her fasten and adjust it on her pale neckline, she reaches up to give me the smallest, saddest peck on my cheek. *I made a wish for you,* she said. Yet I know that that wish was not for my happiness, but for her own.

CHAPTER 27
Julia

I pop another Dorito into my mouth and chew. Since Eron "disappeared," I've eaten almost an entire bag. Salty foods are my comfort, and right now I need all the comfort I can get. Though instead of just feeling weirded out, I now feel weirded out and sick to my stomach, which isn't an improvement.

My fingers are coated in bright orange cheese dust, so I lick them and snuggle under the blankets, hoping a Reese Witherspoon movie will keep my mind occupied. It isn't working.

Eron, before my eyes, *disappeared*. For the second time. Like, *poof*.

So either I am having a mental breakdown, or some really messed-up stuff is going on.

Not only that, he gave me some lame-ass story about being a Sandman. About Griffin being one, too. Since then, I haven't been able to get that song *"Mr. Sandman, bring me a dream . . ."* out of my head. Isn't that what Sandmen are supposed to do? Bring nice, happy dreams to people? Why is mine bringing me nightmares?

Well, if I'm having nightmares because Griffin is behind it, that *does* make sense. Everything's a joke to Griffin. Wherever he is, he's probably laughing, thinking, What other things can I add to her dreams to make her never want to sleep again?

I roll up the bag of chips and toss it onto the floor, then stare up at the corners of the room. Eron said he's watching me.

Could anything possibly be creepier?

All right, I tell myself, straightening on the couch. If he is watching me, then he can hear me. And nobody is home, so if I talk to him out loud and this all turns out to be just some lame practical joke, I won't get carted off to a mental hospital.

"Griffin," I whisper to the air. "Do you hear me?"

Feeling more comfortable, I speak more loudly. "Griffin. You need to cut out whatever you are doing, okay? I care about you, but you're really freaking me out. Okay? So just stop it. Go toward the light."

"Hon?"

I turn to see my mom standing in the door of the living room with a bag of groceries. When did she become a ninja?

"Oh, hi, Mom," I say. "Um, just practicing a play."

I can tell by her face that she doesn't believe me, but I don't think she wants to know what I'm up to, either. She drops the bag on the kitchen table and starts to unpack it. "I bought more Doritos."

"Thanks," I say. If it is possible to OD on Doritos, I am almost there.

"Shouldn't you be in bed?" she asks. "You have your driver's test bright and early tomorrow."

"Um . . ." It's after eleven but all I can think of is Eron's warning. If I see Griffin in my dreams, I need to wake myself up. What if he does come? What if I can't wake up? What will he do? He was my boyfriend, not some crazed lunatic. Although Bret is also one of my best friends—at least, I think he is. I remember Eron's words to me: *People you know, even very well, can surprise you.*

Sigh. I'd rather just *not* sleep and save myself from wetting the bed tonight.

But then I yawn.

And I know that will never work.

CHAPTER 28
Eron

Both Vicki and Evangeline have been asleep for many hours when Julia trudges upstairs, rubbing her eyes. I can sense her trepidation as she pulls back her covers and slips into the bed. I hope that I can make her slumber a comfortable one.

As I'm about to pass into her room, a heavy hand falls on my shoulder, pulling me backward. I lose my balance and slip from the tree, scraping my arms and cheek on branches before landing with a dull thud on the dewy grass. "Mr. Colburn!" I hiss in the darkness.

"Yeah?" he says, dangling above me on a branch.

"What have you been up to?" I shout, standing and brushing off my pants.

He snorts. "I had the same question for you. But I know. Julia's dreams filled me in." He jumps down and stands toe to toe with me. We glare at each other murderously. "She is *mine.*"

I turn back toward her window. "You're crazy."

"You are not going in there!" he whispers fiercely. "If you so much as look at her again, I'll kill you."

I laugh. "I'm still a Sandman, thanks to you. You can no more end my life than I can end yours."

He stands there, shaking with anger. "You said you would protect her. Not steal her from me."

"She can't be stolen from you. She's not yours."

"She *is*! She just doesn't know I'm still here. But when she does—"

"She already knows. I told her."

His eyes narrow. "What else did you tell her? What lies have you been spreading about me?"

"You can't change who you are, not now. Accept who you are, Mr. Colburn."

"Can't do that, old man," he sighs.

And with that, he disappears through Julia's window.

I'm not leaving her. I climb the tree and pass quietly into the room. He's standing over her, his hands spread. "Get away," he whispers as I move closer.

Julia winces and rolls over. I stand against the wall, arms crossed. "I'm not leaving."

Suddenly, Mr. Colburn's image fades into the darkness. I look at my hands. Of course. He has come back to his duties, and now I am human. Human and . . . inside Julia's home. I reach for the window and jam my knuckles against it. I'm trapped here. Now I need to sneak down the stairs and out the front door undetected, or else risk frightening the life out of Julia. I know that wherever he is, Mr. Colburn is probably laughing at me. He is in control now. With Julia asleep, I am powerless.

I give the air where I know Mr. Colburn is standing a stern look, then creep toward the door. As I open it, it creaks. Julia sits up in bed immediately. "Eron?" she says, rubbing her eyes.

I whisper, "I can explain—"

"I can't get Griffin out of my head. He won't leave me alone."

"It's okay, shhh," I say, as soothingly as possible from across the room. With Mr. Colburn there, I have to fight the urge to go to her, to hold her, as fierce as it may be.

She pulls the covers up to her chin. "I don't care how you got here. I'm glad."

I move closer and see that she's trembling. I put my finger to my lips. *He's here,* I mouth.

Her eyes scan the room, narrowing. *Now?* she mouths back to me. I nod. Her angry voice pierces the silence. "Stop, Griffin. I'm serious. *Please.* You know I care about you. But we need to move on."

A picture frame, the one holding a photo of Griffin on Julia's bedside table, topples over. She turns to it, then to me, her face questioning. I imagine Mr. Colburn's anger; I almost *feel* the heat as he seethes in his invisibility. He will not be happy about this, not at all. I reach over to return the picture to its upright position, and that's when she reaches up and pulls me to the bed.

"But Griffin . . . ," I caution her.

"He's always been stubborn. Maybe he needs to *see* I've moved on before he'll believe it," she whispers tentatively.

She doesn't look away. She brings my hand to her cheek and I feel the rough imprint of her scars. "You know how I got these, don't you?"

I nod.

"You probably know more than I do. When I was in the trailer, when I was seven, I was asleep the whole time. . . ." She blinks. "Because of you?"

"Yes."

"I finally remember you being there, in my dreams. You kept me company the whole time. That's why I was never afraid. And you put that horrible man to sleep, so that I could escape?"

"Yes," I say, embarrassed. I try to right myself, but she doesn't let go. Her soft lips touch mine. I realize that this is no accident. This is what she wants.

When she pulls away, I lie there, stunned, before scrambling to my feet. Finally experiencing something he's waited over a hundred years for will do that to a person.

"Did he see that?" she asks me.

"I—I—" I stammer. Perhaps I should be worried that Mr. Colburn will take something to the back of my head, but I am too concerned with trying to steady my weak knees. She *kissed* me. "I am certain he did."

"You have no right to do this to me, Griffin," she yells, her voice more authoritative than I've ever known her to be.

I can still taste her, a flavor like mint and strawberries. Her lips were so soft; I never knew it possible to have lips that soft. Mine are probably sandpaper in comparison. Yet I can't resist moving closer to her, wanting to try again. Obviously Harmon has never experienced this, or he'd never wish to be a Sandman again. I move to the edge of her bed, and she puts her hand over mine. She sinks under the covers and pulls my body to her, and I'm so lost in the swell of my own heartbeat and the heat from her skin that I can do nothing but follow, her willing slave.

"Julia?"

I jump. In the darkness is Mrs. Devine, clad in a pale yellow nightshirt that matches her moonlit complexion.

"Mom?" Julia mumbles.

"What are you doing in here?" she barks, jabbing her finger at me. Then she turns to Julia. "Oh, you are in *so much trouble*, young lady."

I stand there, straight as an arrow. I can just hear Mama groaning her disapproval. In my time, a mother would have had every right to beat a boy senseless over something like this. And I would have applauded her. I bow my head in respect, then follow her out the bedroom door. She seethes at me, and as I'm descending the staircase, I hear her exchanging heated words with her daughter.

Outside, I am trembling in the midnight air. I'm not sure where to go; I don't want to leave her. After a moment, I see Julia watching me from the window. Her cheeks are still red from the lashing she took from her mother. She leans over and whispers, "Will I see you tomorrow?"

"Julia, I'm concerned . . . about Griffin." My teeth chatter as I speak, but it's more from awe than from fear.

"Why? He was my boyfriend. He wouldn't hurt me. . . ." Her voice trails off. I know what is finally dawning on her. *People you know, even very well, can surprise you.*

"Julia, don't sleep. You must do everything you can not to."

She yawns. "I'm so beat. And I have my driver's test tomorrow."

"As long as I am human, Griffin is in charge of putting you to sleep. And I have no idea what he might do."

"What do you mean? How can I . . ." She yawns again.

I wrap my fingers around a low branch of the familiar tree outside her home. When I reach her window, I climb inside, realizing that I've never before worked to keep someone *awake*. But I suppose that these days, I am used to new experiences.

Julia leans against her headboard, pulls her knees up to her chest, and snorts. "I can't believe this. So, like, all this time, we've all had Sandmen putting us to sleep? And we can't sleep without them?"

"Yes."

"Are they always as . . . um, attractive as you are?"

She is blushing, and I feel the blood running to my cheeks as well. "A human's Sandman is always someone they would find physically appealing, yes. It's easier for us that way."

"But what does Griffin have to do with this?"

"He is your Sandman now," I explain. "Our tenure is only one hundred years. My time is almost expired, and I am due to hand my charges to Mr. Colburn shortly."

"Oh, great, the king of practical jokes is my Sandman. Figures," she says, rolling her eyes. "And then what will happen to you?"

"I will be human again."

"Really? Well, now it all makes sense, I guess. Why you act so different, look so different . . . You haven't been human since . . . what? Nineteen ten?"

I nod.

"Are you scared?"

"I was." Up until now.

"Did you really mean what you said about wanting to build buildings?" Julia asks me.

"Yes. My mother took me to see the Flatiron Building when I was ten. I was fascinated."

"My dad was interviewing at grad schools when I was twelve and he took me into the Empire State Building. I loved the Art Deco. From that moment on, I was hooked. I used to build things out of Popsicle sticks," she laughs, pointing at a misshapen square building model in the corner of her room. I remember the hours she spent putting that together, working well into the night, yawning and concentrating under the dim lamplight, until she could no longer fight me off. She pulls off her covers and walks to her bookshelf, which is filled with everything from *Wuthering Heights* to the picture books her mother used to read her every night before bed. She removes a big book, one I've never seen before. "Have you heard of this place?"

I sit on the pale pink carpet, using her bed as a backboard, and she sits next to me, legs crossed. She places the book open in my lap and I gasp. Buildings that defy logic are there. "Are these . . . real?"

She nods, inspecting the pictures as I flip. "It's a place called Dubai, in the Middle East. Over here, there are all these rules you have to follow. But there, architects are given free rein to create whatever crazy building designs they like. Aren't these amazing?"

I gape in wonder. "Amazing" doesn't begin to describe them. Not only are they tall enough to reach the moon, but the shapes are gorgeous. Some look like they are made entirely from mirrors. Others are shaped with soft curves instead of harsh angles. "I've never seen such a thing."

She opens to a page where I'm greeted by the most magnificent structure I have ever seen. "The Burj Khalifa," she says. "Tallest building in the world."

"Can they . . . can they touch the moon from there?" I ask.

She laughs. "Almost. It won't be the tallest for long, though; they keep building them higher and higher. But I want to go there. I want to see them in person."

I nod. At this moment, I do, too.

"I met with a professor when I was applying for the *Architectural Journal* summer session—that's where I'm going this summer—because I wanted to make my application package the best it could be. Most of the other applicants are high school seniors or college freshmen, so I knew it was a long shot," she explains. "And he told me something that Winston Churchill once said. 'We shape our buildings; thereafter, they shape us.' There are few professions where you can influence people in a positive way like that."

I assume Winston Churchill must be a famous architect. "Yes, I would much rather add to this world than take away from it."

"Exactly." She closes the book and studies me. "You have been with me my whole life, haven't you?"

I nod. "Does that bother you?"

She shrugs. "It's a little creepy. But kind of cool, I guess. You're like my guardian angel."

"Oh, no," I say, pressing my back against her bed. "I'm not quite as powerful as that. And I wouldn't want you—I don't know—trying to fly from a bridge because you think I can save you."

She raises an eyebrow. "You can't?"

I shake my head.

"Then what good are you?" she says in mock disappointment, and then laughs. "Tell me about the Sandmen. Everything."

I take a breath and prepare for a long story. But I suppose we have all night. "Where shall I start?"

CHAPTER 29
Julia

"**Y**ou're more than grounded for life, you know," my mom says with a snort as we pull into the DMV's driver testing course. "We're nailing the windows shut. How irresponsible can you be? You're lucky we're still taking you for your license."

I'm still thinking about Eron, so my mom's words don't register. When I was three, I accidentally stuck my finger into an outlet and got a shock, but this is like a thousand times more intense. My lips still tremble when I think of it. And I am the one who started it. Me. I always let Griffin lead me around, dictate what happened next. Now I am in control. I like that. "That's fine," I say solemnly, not sure what I'm agreeing to. "I am very sorry."

She pats her purse nervously and sticks her foot on the dashboard again when I pull rather quickly

into an open parking spot. "And to think I'm sending you off on your own in a couple weeks."

"I thought you said I can take care of myself," I say.

She snorts. "Well, I thought so, until last night."

We walk into the DMV and I hand my forms and identification to the lady at the desk. She smiles and says, "Just go on and have a seat over there. Someone will be with you shortly."

I smile at a couple of fidgety girls. One is sitting on the edge of her seat, looking like she might fall off, and the other is bouncing her knee so quickly that her flip-flop keeps making a smack-smack-smack noise against the bottom of her foot. My mom picks up a driver's manual—which, while not exactly *Redbook,* is the only reading around—and starts to page through it. I just sit beside her, yawn, and rifle through my purse for some gum.

I find some orange-flavored gum and offer a piece to the girls next to me. They decline. I shove a piece into my mouth and yawn again.

And again.

It's got to be the fluorescent lighting and the dull walls. Why can't these places ever look more exciting? It's like they hope to scare people away. I close my eyes and realize that's what they want. To be closed. To stay that way.

"Is there a Coke machine here?" I ask my mom.

She shrugs. "You might try getting enough sleep instead of—"

"Mom, I slept fine. I'm just thirsty," I groan, standing. I walk around the room until I find a line of vending machines. I see Mountain Dew. Eureka. I pop in my quarters and drink it down. Better. I stand there, reading some boring signs on the wall about child restraint laws and penalties for DUI, because even that is more exciting than being near my mom.

Suddenly, my mom nudges me. Somehow, without even knowing how I got here, I'm sitting next to her again. The two girls are gone. My soda can is empty in my hand. I can't remember taking the walk back from the vending machines. "What the . . . ," I begin.

"You're up," my mom says. She must be at a really good part of her manual, because she doesn't glance up. There is a chubby man waiting in the doorway. He looks sort of like the Michelin Man, but in plaid, and not as cute or happy. This man looks a little like someone spit in his morning coffee. Great. Before I know it, my bag slips from my hands, its contents spilling onto the ground with a clatter.

Michelin Man doesn't move, but my mom reaches down and grabs my cell. She studies me. "Are you okay?"

I nod. "Oh, sure. Fine." I summon every last bit of my energy to prove the point. I jump up and put on my most confident smile.

"Good luck, hon," she says.

"Hi," I say brightly, bounding up to meet the man.

He grunts and just keeps staring at his clipboard. "Miss Devine."

"Yes, that's me."

He grunts again and leads me outside to the back of the building, where there are three identical Ford compact cars waiting. It's a hot day but my palms begin to sweat even before the chill of the air-conditioning has worn off. I'm suddenly aware I have to pee—obviously, since I just downed an entire can of Dew. I yawn again, a long one, and I can't shut my mouth for the life of me. Of course, that's when the man looks at me. I try to

stretch it into an open-mouthed smile, but that doesn't work. His frown deepens.

He motions me to the middle Ford and hands me the keys. I walk around to the driver's side and sit in the seat. It's not very comfortable, so I attempt to adjust it, pretending like I am an old pro at this even though I have no idea how the seat works. In the silence of the car, I notice that Michelin Man has a problem with breathing. His breath is so loud it sounds like my dad's snoring. How can anyone concentrate on their driving around him? After I fiddle with the seat for a few minutes, he finally lets out a sound like *snarf* from the back of his throat and reaches under my seat. It slides backward easily. By that time, we've been in the car with the windows up for five minutes and it's like an inferno. My bangs are sweat-glued to my face.

I put the key in the ignition, turn it. The car starts up. The sun beats down through the windshield. I can't help it: I yawn again. The man clucks his tongue. I wrap my fingers around the hot steering wheel and pray to the caffeine gods for my Mountain Dew to kick in.

"Please pull out and drive to the third cone."

I check my mirrors, then press gently on the accelerator. *Twinge.*

The car bucks. What was that?

I will my eyes to stay open, but I feel the lids sliding shut.

Oh, no.

And that's when I see Griffin.

CHAPTER 30
Eron

"**A**re you angry at me?"

I blink. I'm standing on the edge of a cliff, looking down at the black waves as they crash upon the rocks below. Chimere is beside me.

"What is this?" I ask. "Where am I?"

She smiles. "You're dreaming."

"I'm . . . sleeping?"

"Yes, you are human. You are my charge. I lured you here. Remember? Just like in the old days."

"Oh." It's been a long time since I've been in this state, unconscious, unaware. From the moment I left Julia's house early this morning, things became fuzzy. I can't recall what I did after I climbed quietly out her window as the sun stretched above the horizon. I'm thankful that the kiss hasn't disappeared from my memory. Neither has the feeling of lying next to her, really lying next to her, with her head on my shoulder for hours on end. I wiggle my fingers and feel the nubby worn fabric of Harmon's old couch. Somehow, I'd made it there. "But if I am human, then Mr. Colburn . . ."

"That is why I lured you here; so that I might speak to you." Her eyes turn troubled. "Mr. Colburn has disappeared once again."

I shake my head. Of course. Did I expect any different? Then I realize that something is peculiar about this instance. "If he is neglecting his duties and not performing the seduction, shouldn't I be a Sandman?"

"Yes, that is what troubles me."

I back away from the edge of the cliff, pondering. Chimere wrings her hands; I can tell she already knows what this means, and she's none too pleased. "What does it mean, then?"

Her voice is mouse-like. "That he's still performing his duties."

I squint at her. "You mean . . . he may be attempting to seduce her to sleep? Now?"

"Yes."

"He's going to try to hurt her."

She nods. "I am afraid so."

I remember what she said to me last night. *I have my driver's test tomorrow.* Driver's test. I grab Chimere by the shoulders. "I need to wake up. The sand . . ."

"I only did enough for a catnap," she answers, her eyes downcast. "You may wake yourself easily."

I smile sadly at her. I know that if she wanted to serve her own selfish motives, she could very well have let Griffin carry on, fail in his duties, so that I would be forced to be a Sandman forever. But Chimere is and always has been, above all, a Sleepbringer. My protector. I reach out and stroke the smooth skin of her jaw. "You're wonderful," I say, and the last thing I can recall from the dream is the way she takes my hand in her own, clearly savoring the feeling of my skin against hers.

I concentrate on something real—the fabric of the couch. I dig my fingers into it, hard, then quickly pull myself out of sleep. I open my eyes and the first thing I focus on is the lazily spinning ceiling fan. My head is thick, my eyesight bleary. I stand, try to catch my bearings.

Julia.

Some confusing moments later, after inquiring with nearly a dozen people on the street and receiving conflicting information as to where this "driver testing facility" is, I race down the shoulder of the highway, avoiding the automobiles that are honking their horns at me. The parking lot is full; the Devine family automobile, now repaired, is parked in it, but there is no sign of Julia.

I call her name as I rush toward the building, and that is when I hear the screech of tires. I turn toward an empty concrete lot in the distance and see a small white automobile swerving around a bend. I can just make out Julia's head— the low ponytail, the pale skin—in the driver's-side window.

I cup my hands around my mouth. "Julia!"

The car is moving closer. I can see her white knuckles on the wheel, and I can also now see her eyes.

They flutter closed.

She is asleep.

The automobile skids through a stop sign, and when the right tire hits a curb, the car is momentarily airborne. It strikes the ground hard, then barrels straight across the lot, toward a busy intersection. Paralyzed, I watch as it swerves again, this time racing at breakneck speed, directly toward me.

The heat and dust rise off the pavement surrounding the vehicle, but in the blurred distance beyond, I'm almost positive I see Mr. Colburn. And he's smiling.

CHAPTER 31
Julia

In the haze, Griffin smiles at me. It's not his usual, wicked smile, laced with mischief. It's sad. Desperate.

"What are you doing here?" I ask him.

"I came for you."

"That's sweet. But in case you didn't notice, I'm kind of busy. I'm . . ." I pause, look around. Everything but Griffin's body is enveloped in white smoke. The same smoke must be clouding my brain, because I can't recall what I was doing before I noticed him. "I can't remember what I'm doing, but it's important."

He's wearing the tuxedo he wore for prom. The one he's been wearing in every dream I've had of him lately. It still looks uncomfortable and stiff on him, even when he leans back and crosses his arms behind his head. "Talk to me, okay?"

I sigh. "All right." I step

next to him. He clears a space in the smoke and I sit beside him. "About what?"

"Things." He scratches his chin, thinking hard, which reminds me: we never talked before. Not really. We just traded jabs, like in a never-ending boxing match. That's probably why he pulls out the most generic, impersonal question you can ask someone: "How have you been?"

"I'm fine," I answer, wondering why Griffin is so not Griffin. And why does it feel like I haven't spoken to him in weeks? Suddenly, I remember. "Are you still dead?"

"Sort of. I'm a Sandman," he tells me. "I put people to sleep. It's cool."

"Oh?" I seem to remember hearing someone tell me about Sandmen before. I can't remember who it was. Someone else . . .

"Yeah. I sort of . . . miss you, Jules. I want you to be with me."

He's raising his eyebrows, pleading, sincere. This is all too *Twilight Zone* for me. Since when has Griffin Colburn been sincere? When has he ever pleaded with me for anything? Stooped to say he missed me? All I can manage is "Oh."

"Don't you miss me? Don't you love me?"

Okay, where is the *real* Griffin Colburn? He's never asked me a question like that; he never needed to. "Sure . . . yeah."

"Then come with me." He wraps his hand around mine. It's cool, smoother than I remember, as if all the imperfections have been washed away. Or maybe I don't remember his hand very well, because we rarely held hands, rarely touched in any intimate way, unless he was trying to round the bases.

He looks me in the eye, really looks at me. And it's listening to him say such sweet things, feeling his soft touch, that makes me yearn for more. This is everything we were missing. This is what I always wanted. This will make things perfect. I mouth, *Yes.*

"Julia, don't!"

I turn my head to the voice. It's familiar, but far away. In the distance, I see him.

Eron.

Suddenly, I remember. Something pounds at my temples. Fear. I was afraid of Griffin. I turn to him. His face is more desperate, and his hands feel colder and damp in mine. He is trying to keep his eyes focused on mine, but something new is appearing there. Rage.

I stand, back away, despite his trying to lace his fingers with mine. I snatch them away. "What are you doing?"

"Wake up, Julia!"

Griffin stands and takes a step toward me. "Don't listen—"

"Wake up!"

I pull myself into consciousness, shuddering as I pry open my eyes and see my hands wrapped around a steering wheel. Steering wheel? A heavy body pushes me against the door; it's the instructor, sleeping, his cheek pressed against my shoulder. We were both sleeping . . . and driving? Beyond the steering wheel are the blacktop, sparkling and blurred in the sunlight, and a line of trees, which we're quickly rushing up to meet. And before that . . . a figure of a man. He's too blurry to recognize, but he's all in black, melting into the pavement. His hands are outstretched, mouth curved in an O.

And I'm heading right for him. I stomp on the brake, too late. I hit with a dull thud. Bits of glass, like snowflakes, scatter over me, piercing my skin. I taste blood. The car begins to fishtail. Everything goes white, then black.

Someone is screaming. Another familiar voice. Mine.

The car shrieks to a halt. My fingers are doughy and numb as I reach for the door handle, but I pull it open and scramble to stand. In the distance, people are yelling, emerging from the DMV building as if it were on fire. The path where the car was is clear except for two tire marks burned on the ground. Speckles of glass are everywhere, crunching underfoot. Maybe I imagined it. Maybe it was all some horrible dream.

Then I see the body, motionless, on the other side of the car. His head is tilted to the sky, almost as if he's sunbathing, but his body is twisted to the side unnaturally.

I rush to him. The first things I see are blood and a huge gash in his forehead. "Eron?" I ask softly, placing a hand gently on his shoulder. Even the slant of his shoulder seems unnatural, as if all the parts of his body are broken. He doesn't move, doesn't answer.

What have I done?

CHAPTER 32
Eron

It's as if the car passes right through me. There is no pain.

Colburn has broken the rules, and I'm a Sandman again. Colburn is laughing in the distance. I rush up to him and grab him by the shoulders so that he collapses, and for a moment, I hold him by his tuxedo jacket, pinning him to the ground. I am no match for his brawn, but I manage to grind him hard into the pavement. He moans in pain. He quickly rolls me over, and he brings a heavy fallen branch to my neck. He pushes against my throat, hard.

"Mr. Colburn!" a voice calls. Chimere's. "I've had enough of this."

She rushes to us, and the next thing I know, he is straightening, stumbling toward her. He falls into her arms. Beyond them, I see Julia scrambling over to my body. My human body.

Am I . . . ?

"She belongs with me, she belongs with me," Colburn is muttering.

"Let her go," Chimere whispers to him. I am entranced by the girl bending over my body. Julia leans in, very gently touching me. I haven't been injured so badly since that day in the textile mill when I lost my arm and my life. Julia wipes the blood from my eye with her long, delicate fingers. She's rocking back and forth slightly. And doing something I haven't seen her do in many years.

Crying.

I walk toward her, stand over her small crumpled body. I want badly to touch her and tell her it's all right, I'm fine. But am I?

I turn to Chimere. "What am I doing there?" I ask, confused. My human body is there, yet I'm still a Sandman. How can I be in two places at once?

She sniffs. "You were human again, my pet. Completely. For the briefest time."

"And now?"

She turns to Griffin. "Now it is up to Mr. Colburn to assume your place. If he cannot . . ."

"Let me go to her," I say to Griffin, my voice insistent.

"I . . . can't," Colburn says burying his head in his arms.

"We can." Chimere leans into him, and I can just make out her words. "I will let Eron go, if you let go of Julia."

He raises his chin and studies her. Finally, he nods almost imperceptibly.

"Promise?" Chimere grins at him and wraps her arm tightly around him.

"Yeah. I promise," he says.

She wraps her other arm around him and pulls his head to her heart. Holding him, she smiles at me, not unkindly, and motions me toward Julia. Then she leans into his ear and says, "Don't be troubled, my pet."

CHAPTER 33
Julia

I lug the last of my suitcases out to the trunk of the RAV4 and nearly collapse in exhaustion on the back bumper.

"I do wish you'd let me help you."

I laugh. "Sure. Whatever."

Eron is leaning against the garage door, arms crossed, glaring down at his crutches, which he's thrown aside for the hundredth time today. "Those dreaded things. I am not an invalid."

"Right," I say.

He pulls himself up from leaning and attempts to walk toward me but ends up hopping. The cast on his lower leg is big. I pick up the crutches and hand them to him. Finally, he relents and puts one under each arm. "Dreaded things," he mutters.

I suppose we're both limited in our modes of travel. Eron can barely walk, and I failed my driver's test. Obviously. Though my mother wasn't happy with my performance that day, she is glad I won't be driving around the streets of New York City. And she thinks there are worse boyfriends to have than a guy who's so polite he makes Miss Manners weep with joy. And even though he has a penchant for showing up in my bedroom late at night, he likes her gazpacho, so in her eyes, it balances out.

"I'll see you in a week," I tell him, smiling under the weight of his gaze. I can't not smile when looking at him, can't not feel warm and shivery at the same time.

He nods.

"And I'll call you when I get settled in."

"All right."

"And before I go to bed, okay?"

"Yes."

"And in the morning."

He laughs at me. "That would be lovely."

I bite my lip. "I hope the bed isn't lumpy. You know how I like my sleep."

"I do, all too well," he says. He reaches over, cups my face in his hands, and kisses me long and slow on the lips. My toes curl. "I wish you sweet dreams."

I smile. *That's what you are. My sweetest dream, come true.*

CYN BALOG had a massive case of insomnia while writing *Sleepless*. She lives in Pennsylvania with her husband and daughters. Visit her online at www.cynbalog.com.